W9-BUO-586

When Baldwin Loved Brenden

Electa Rome Parks

Margaret E. Heggan Public Library
606 Delsea Drive
Sewell, NJ 08080

www.urbanbooks.net

Urban Books, LLC
78 East Industry Court
Deer Park, NY 11729

When Baldwin Loved Brenden © 2013
Electa Rome Parks

All rights reserved. No part of this book may be reproduced in any form or by any means without prior consent of the Publisher, except brief quotes used in reviews.

ISBN 13: 978-1-60162-376-8
ISBN 10: 1-60162-376-3

First Trade Paperback Printing February 2013
Printed in the United States of America

10 9 8 7 6 5 4 3 2 1

This is a work of fiction. Any references or similarities to actual events, real people, living or dead, or to real locales are intended to give the novel a sense of reality. Any similarity in other names, characters, places, and incidents is entirely coincidental.

Distributed by Kensington Publishing Corp.
Submit Wholesale Orders to:
Kensington Publishing Corp.
C/O Penguin Group (USA) Inc.
Attention: Order Processing
405 Murray Hill Parkway
East Rutherford, NJ 07073-2316
Phone: 1-800-526-0275
Fax: 1-800-227-9604

When Baldwin Loved Brenden

by

Electa Rome Parks

Dedication

Dedicated to all on a journey of self-discovery and enlightenment.

Epigraph

However rare true love may be, it is less so than true friendship.

– Francois de La Rochefoucauld

Acknowledgments

When something is for you, there's a feeling that is deep down inside of you that will not allow you to let it go.

– Tyler Perry

That's what writing is, was, and will forever and always be for me. Something that speaks directly to my soul. A vehicle that allows me to have a voice like no other. My love affair. My peace.

I don't know what the future holds. . . . To quote Oprah Winfrey, "What I know for sure: No matter where you are on your journey, that's exactly where you need to be. The next road is always ahead." My destiny remains to be seen.

To my readers, whom I affectionately refer to as family, many of you have been on this journey with me from the very beginning. And others joined the journey many miles and mile markers down the road. Others have just recently joined the trip. The road traveled hasn't always been smooth, but paved with bumps and valleys along the way, but through it all, you've been my loyal passengers. For that I will be eternally grateful. To you, to all of you, I say thank you! Thank you from the bottom of my heart for helping this black girl to live out her dream. I have so appreciated the show of support, the encouragement, the kind words of praise, the spirit of sisterhood, and the sense of bonding experienced through the written word. You've been the magic in my life.

Thank you to the many book clubs, bookstores, online sites, social media outlets, authors, and organizations that have shown me love over the years. You guys are the best, and I will never forget it. You have touched my heart.

As I've said from book one, *The Ties That Bind*, up until now, with the novel you hold in your hands, *When Baldwin Loved Brenden*, all I've ever wanted to do was write. Just write. Simply write.

I didn't sign up for all the extra.

So, until the next book brings us together again, stay blessed. Live your life to the fullest, because life is short. Embrace it with all you have, because you don't get a second chance. This is not the dress rehearsal; this is the actual play. Find yourself. Be happy. As for me, I'm going wherever my journey takes me next. Keep in touch at novelideal@aol.com, and don't be a stranger!

Peace & abundant blessings,
Electa

Signing off: Atlanta, GA, June 16, 2012, 1:42 A.M.
novelideal@aol.com
www.electaromeparks.com
www.facebook.com/electaromeparks
www.electaromeparks.blogspot.com

P.S. Please support my previous titles: *The Ties That Bind, Loose Ends, Almost Doesn't Count, Ladies' Night Out, These Are My Confessions, Diary of a Stalker, True Confessions,* and *The Stalker Chronicles.* Kindly continue to post those reviews.

Prologue

I'm not going to lie. . . . I'm scared. I'm more afraid than I have ever been in my entire life. I know it won't be long now, and I don't even try to fool myself into thinking otherwise. I can feel my soul preparing to leave my body, but I'm ready. I'm tired, so tired of fighting. I've fought the good fight for as long as I mentally and physically can.

My body is worn out, battered beyond repair, and simply can't take any more radiation and chemotherapy treatment. Now it's time to throw in the white flag and quietly surrender in the midst of the storm. I've won other battles over the last two years, but I'll lose this war, and I'm at peace with that. I made peace a while back. I'm at peace with myself and at peace with my God. I'm not sad, so don't feel sorry for me. That would be such an injustice to my memory.

I have lived a good life, experienced most of what I've wanted to, and most of all, I've had the opportunity to meet some wonderful people during my lifetime. People I'm honored to call my friends, but I've learned that friends can let you down. However, that's life and we are all human. None of us are perfect. Translation: we make mistakes.

I wish I could have carried out our reunion, but I'm afraid my time has run out. Run out. That's funny; I keep picturing one of those old-fashioned hourglasses. You know the ones I'm talking about; they have two glass bulbs connected vertically, allowing a controlled trickle of material from the top to the bottom. Once the top bulb is empty, the hourglass can be inverted to begin measuring time again. Yet I can't be inverted to start all over again.

I probably won't live to see Baldwin, Brenden, Bria, and Christopher again, not in this lifetime. That's a shame, because I'll never have the opportunity to thank them for what a difference they made in my life years ago and they didn't even know it. When it was all said and done, all that other stuff didn't even matter. I finally learned not to sweat the small stuff.

Maybe from my death they'll learn that life is too short, so embrace it with all you have, because you don't get a second chance. This is not the dress rehearsal; this is the actual play.

Rihanna

Chapter 1

Baldwin

Friday evening, as soon as I unlocked the front door, juggling my purse and briefcase on one shoulder, and walked into my ranch-style home after a long day and an even longer week at work, the ringing telephone grated my nerves to no end. I thought I was one of the few people I knew who still had a landline. And I used it. I knew the caller couldn't be William, my boyfriend of almost two years, since he was out of town on one of his regular monthly business trips, and besides, I had talked to him earlier on my cell during my tedious Atlanta rush-hour drive home.

Whoever was on the other end had no plans of hanging up anytime soon. I reluctantly walked the short distance to the small decorative table to answer the call. All I could think about was immersing myself in a hot, relaxing jasmine bubble bath as I sipped on a glass of wine and melted my stress away, with an entire weekend to look forward to.

"Hello," I said, trying my best to keep mild annoyance out of the tone of my voice. It had better not be a telemarketer trying to persuade me to purchase a new product or try out some upgraded service or donate to a charity. I was on the Georgia No Call list for a reason.

"May I speak with Baldwin Sparks please?" the caller asked.

"This is she," I volunteered, still trying to figure out why the voice sounded familiar, yet I couldn't quite place it.

"Baldwin. It's me, girl. Bria," the caller literally had screamed into the phone. "How have you been?"

"Uh, fine," I murmured, still in shock over hearing a voice from my past. At one point in my life, Bria and I were as close as sisters, maybe even closer. The fantasy world of college ended all too soon, and we were quickly swept up into the reality of life and careers and bills, separated from one another in our quest for greatness. Bria stayed in North Carolina, and I moved back to Georgia.

"Girl, is that all you can say after all these years?" She laughed. It was still that high-pitched, bubbly squeal I remembered so vividly. Bria and I had shared many late-night giggling sessions, some lasting into the early morning hours. We'd be doubled over, laughing so hard our stomachs ached as we clutched them.

"I guess you caught me by surprise, that's all. I haven't talked to you and the rest of the group in, like, forever."

"Tell me about it. That's a damn shame too," she stated, with a hint of sadness clinging to her voice. "We all lost contact with one another, slowly but surely. Simply drifted apart. Yet we were close, almost like a small dysfunctional family. If the walls could talk." She laughed lightly at her own joke.

I remained silent as memories flooded my mind, mostly happy ones. The others I chose to ignore because I couldn't bear them.

"Listen, hopefully we can reminisce later. Unfortunately, I'm afraid I'm calling with bad news," Bria sighed. "I hate to be the one to share this."

"Share what? What is it?" I asked cautiously, bracing myself.

She sighed again, not ready to be the bearer of bad news.

I held my breath, hoped for the best, and braced for the worse.

"Rihanna passed away Wednesday."

I gasped. "What? No! What happened?" I questioned, finally dropping my soft leather tan briefcase on the floor, releasing my purse near the sofa, and heavily sitting down because my feet could no longer support me.

"Rihanna had terminal breast cancer, had been battling it for two years. I heard she put up one hell of a fight too."

"I didn't know," I said in a near whisper. "I never knew," I whispered as tears threatened to spill from my eyes.

"None of us did. I spoke with Christopher and Brenden yesterday. I had a harder time finding you during my Internet search, so I couldn't reach you until today."

At the mention of Brenden's name, my mouth went dry like I had stuffed cotton into it and my heartbeat sped up. Suddenly, I felt light-headed, and I thought for a second I was going to pass out. I leaned back against my sofa. I had wrongly assumed that after all these years I had finally gotten him out of my system. For good.

"Are you there?" Bria asked. "Baldwin?"

"Yes. I'm here," I somehow managed to murmur.

"I spoke with them after Rihanna's mother called me."

"Her mom called you? Mrs. Brown?"

"Uh-huh. She confessed Rihanna knew she might not make it and she left us in her will."

"Us?" I inquired.

"You, me, Christopher, and Brenden."

Again, I felt the frantic flutters as I gripped the receiver tighter and closed my eyes to stop the stars that danced merrily before them.

"Oh my God!"

"I know, girl. It's surreal, isn't it?"

"Yeah, to put it mildly. What else did Mrs. Brown say?" I asked.

"Well, the funeral is Wednesday afternoon. Rihanna's mom would like for us to attend and stay through Friday for the reading of the last will and testament."

"Are you serious?" I asked.

"Very. Mrs. Brown has extended Rihanna's home as a place for us to stay. Said Rihanna would want it that way. Everyone else has agreed to come to pay their last respects. You're the last to confirm."

I hesitated for only a brief second, because I clearly recalled numerous times when Rihanna had been there for me in a moment of need. There had been only one time when she wasn't. I had to say my good-byes.

"Okay," I said, trying to clear my head and make sense of the emotions I was experiencing.

"Can you get here by Tuesday? I can pick you up at Raleigh-Durham airport."

"Sure, I guess. That shouldn't be a problem. Give me your cell number, and I'll call you back with my flight info and itinerary as soon as I finalize them."

"Sounds good, Baldwin. I can't wait to see you. I hate that it's under these circumstances, but it really has been too long. Believe it or not, regardless of my actions or inactions, I've missed you. Missed all you guys. It's going to be so strange being together as a group again, especially without Rihanna, our very own mother hen, as we used to call her. Remember that?"

I laughed. "Yeah, I do. How could I forget how she was always cooking, fussing over us and worrying like a mother hen keeping her chicks in line?"

I smiled faintly at the recollection. I had other, not so good ones that threatened to burst loose, but I quickly pushed them back into the deep corners of my mind, because I wasn't ready to recall those. Not yet.

A few minutes later I hung up the phone with a sense of trepidation, sadness, and excitement all rolled into one. What had I gotten myself into? As I reclined on the sofa, I couldn't seem to get my emotions in check. They were all over the place. One minute I felt like crying over the hand life had dealt Rihanna, and seconds later I giggled out loud at some of the memories I recalled.

I hadn't set foot in North Carolina in over ten years, nor had I set eyes on *him* in just as long. When proudly I walked across the stage on graduation day and firmly shook the president's hand, I was determined to put North Carolina and Brenden behind me. Up until now, I had succeeded, but it looked like that was all about to change.

Chapter 2

Brenden

"Bye, Daddy," my nine-year-old son yelled, racing into his room to play with the new electronic game I had bought him over the weekend at GameStop.

"Bye, buddy. I'll call you later this week. I love you. Be good."

"Love you too, Dad," he shouted without looking back once. A thick lump formed in my throat. It was always hard dropping him off after spending a fun-filled weekend together.

My soon-to-be ex-wife stood in the living room with her arms crossed above her ample chest, sucking her teeth. My smile immediately vanished. I had learned that Malia tended to suck all the joy out of any room she happened to be in, and the people who were in it with her.

"What now?" I asked. "What's wrong this time?"

"Brenden, I've told you time and again about buying Jordan new toys every weekend you have him. You are going to spoil that boy rotten. Damn."

"Well, he's my son, and I like spoiling him."

"He's my son too," she said with a serious scowl.

"Malia, I wasn't implying that he wasn't. You see, this is why I can't communicate with you. You make a big deal out of every damn thing," I stated, throwing up my hands.

She shrugged and kept her lips pressed tightly together, her usual mode of disgruntlement.

"I won't be in town for the next few days. So if there is an emergency or you need to get in touch with me regarding Jordan, call me on my cell."

"Where are you going? On another business trip?"

"No. I received a phone call from an old college friend, and unfortunately, she had bad news to share. Rihanna passed away, and I'm attending her funeral in North Carolina."

"Rihanna? Rihanna. That name sounds familiar. Oh yeah. Wasn't she the fat chick you used to hang around with? She was part of your little so-called group."

"Yeah, she was part of the group, though I wouldn't describe her in that way."

"Oh, please! Why not? She was fat, Brenden."

"There was much more to Rihanna than her weight. If you had gotten to know her, she could have taught you a thing or two about dealing with people, being respectful, and treating them with kindness. You don't even have respect for the dead."

"Whatever, Brenden," Malia said, showing me the palm of her hand as she pushed it toward my face.

"Like I said, you'll be able to reach me on my cell phone if Jordan needs me," I said, hastily reaching for the doorknob. I couldn't wait to get out of there. Lately, Malia and I couldn't be in a room with one another for more than a few minutes.

"Wait, Brenden."

I slowly counted to three, stopped, and turned. I waited and simply stared at her.

"Will she be there?"

"Who?"

"You know damn well who I'm talking about. Baldwin." She spat the name as if it hurt even to speak it.

"I have no idea, Malia."

"Uh-huh. Don't forget what you promised me. You said you'd consider giving our marriage another chance, for Jordan's sake."

As I swiftly walked to my car, working on my marriage, the one that had essentially been over for years, was the last thing on my mind. All I could think about was a brown-skinned girl with a beautiful smile, one I hadn't seen since she broke my heart into a million pieces years earlier. Her name was Baldwin.

Margaret E. Heggan Public Library
606 Delsea Drive
Sewell, NJ 08080

Chapter 3

Christopher

"Baby, are you going to miss me while I'm gone?" I asked. We had just finished making love, and now we were basking in the afterglow. I was mellow and content.

"I might," Tamara teased. "The question is, are you going to be a good boy while you're gone?"

"Of course, baby, and I'll think of your lovely face each and every day."

"Yeah, right. I love you with all my heart, Christopher. I really do, but I can't get over how many times you have hurt me in the past by messing with some random woman. I've been a fool far too many times, and I can forgive, but I don't forget."

"Tamara, I'm going to prove to you that I've changed if it kills me. Believe me, baby, when I say you are the only one for me."

"Why haven't you ever mentioned your friend before?" she questioned.

I shrugged. "I don't know. It seems like that time in my life was so long ago. I was a much different person, and at the end, before we went our separate ways, a lot of things happened that scarred our friendship."

"Why even bother to attend the funeral if you haven't seen or talked to her in years?"

"It's hard to explain since you never met Rihanna, but she had a beautiful spirit. Back then, the group had a bond that was everlasting, and I have to attend to show my respects," I said, pulling her close and kissing her forehead.

"The group?" Tamara asked.

"Yeah, that's what we called ourselves. Not much creativity there, huh? There were actually five of us who were the best of friends during our college years. Inseparable. All of us totally different in personality. I never quite understood how we gravitated toward one another to begin with, but we did."

"Interesting. I wish I could go with you for support, sweetie, but you know I have to stay behind to work on that big project at the office. Now would not be the time to leave, because this next promotion is mine. It has my name stamped all over it." She smiled and my world felt brighter. "How does this sound? Tamara Ross, vice president of marketing."

"Sounds wonderful, and you'll get it too. You deserve it."

"See? That's why I couldn't stop loving you even if I tried," she said, reaching to pull me into a hug and give me a passionate kiss.

"Just promise me you'll at least consider my marriage proposal."

"I will, Christopher. I've been thinking about it. Just promise me you won't screw around while you're in North Carolina with the first attractive female that catches your eye."

"Baby, I'm going to a funeral."

"So. Women attend funerals. In fact, are any of these other so-called friends female?"

"Two are, but we didn't roll like that. It was strictly platonic, and they were like the bratty sisters I never had."

"If you say so," Tamara said, turning her back to me and turning off the lamp that sat on the nightstand on her side of the bed. "Get some rest, sweetie. From my experiences, funerals tend to bring out the best and the worst in people."

As she drifted off to sleep, my mind went back in time to the one woman I could never conquer. She would be at the funeral too.

Chapter 4

Bria

"I don't know why you feel it's so important for you to attend this funeral," my baby said, changing into black-and-white workout gear in our bedroom. I lay on our queen-sized bed, hands behind my head, enjoying the view.

"I have to be there. I honestly couldn't think of not going. Rihanna was the sweetest and most genuine person I have ever met," I gushed.

"You said yourself that this group hasn't been together since you all graduated and went your separate ways. That was a long time ago."

"True."

"Don't you think it's going to be uncomfortable spending days cooped up in a house together? They are virtual strangers to you now."

No, Terry. I don't. Like I said, it's hard to explain, but I need to see these people. It's time," I said with conviction.

"Okay. You do what you have to do, but I have to go to the gym right now. You know I missed last week, and I can't miss another day, because I will begin to feel out of sorts."

"Go. Work that fabulous body out for me. When you come back, I'll have a nice dinner prepared with a bottle of red wine, and I'll have a tub run so you can take a relaxing bath before dinner. How does that sound?"

"Hmmm, that sounds wonderful. You are too good to me," Terry said, kissing me fully on the lips and palming my ass.

"You are worth it," I volunteered, winking.

"I love you."

"I adore you." And I meant every word.

As soon as I heard the front door close, my thoughts immediately went back to the group. I walked downstairs to prepare a garden salad and spaghetti with ground turkey and my secret sauce. I had much to share with them, and I was looking forward to seeing the people who I once considered my closest friends, even though we hadn't seen each other in years.

The death of Rihanna was the reason for this mini reunion, but there was something I had been wanting and waiting to tell them for years. So now was finally my chance. I would have them under one roof—a captive audience.

Chapter 5

Baldwin

True friendship continues to grow, even over the longest distance. Same goes for true love.

"Damn, baby! You feel so good."

I threw in a few more moans and groans for good measure as I absently stared at the off-white ceiling of my master bedroom. I secretly wished he hadn't spent the night with me. I had too much on my mind.

"You just don't know what you do to me. Do you? I've been thinking about getting some of this all day," William declared from his position between my spread legs, in between forceful thrusts.

"Come on, sweetie. You're almost there," I cooed, trying to finish up our lovemaking session for the night. I had too much on my mind, and I simply wanted it over. "That's right. Oh, you're hitting my spot. Yes, right there," I softly moaned as I squeezed his firm buttocks a few times and pretended to squirm beneath him.

After two years of dating, I knew when William was about to release himself inside me. His body would tense up, his breathing would become raspy, and he'd speed up his rhythm, almost to a frantic pace. Sure enough, five more minutes passed and he was finished. He kissed me lightly on the lips, rolled over onto his stomach, and was out like a light ten minutes later, lightly snoring.

Typically, I'd be upset that he didn't hold me, spoon with me, and make pillow talk. This time, to be honest, I was grateful for the reprieve, because it gave me a moment to contemplate my trip the next day and to mentally prepare myself.

For most of the night, I tossed and turned, tangled myself in the crisp cotton sheets, as images from my past invaded my slumber and played out as if they had happened yesterday. Finally, at six o'clock I couldn't take it any longer, so I simply got up. Pulling back the bedcovers, which were half on, half off the bed, I quietly crept into the kitchen to enjoy my first morning cup of black coffee. I couldn't start the day any other way. Caffeine was my one vice, and drinking a cup of mocha was part of my daily routine. Without it, I was useless.

"Good morning, baby," William said from the entryway to the kitchen about thirty minutes later.

He hadn't bothered to cover himself and was still nude from the night before. I secretly thought he was an exhibitionist, but he'd never admit to it. He took great pride in his body and went for a sixty-minute jog before work almost each and every morning. At just under six feet, clean-cut, with a dark chocolate, muscular body, he possessed physical attractiveness and intelligence to boot. He was the ideal man for most women. However, lately I had started to have nagging doubts about our relationship and future together.

"Good morning, sweetie," I said as he walked over and gently kissed me, nuzzling my neck. I couldn't help but notice what was already expanding in size between his legs as it swung back and forth.

"Have you taken your multivitamins yet?" he asked.

"No, not yet." I wanted to say, "Not ever." William had insisted that I get in the habit of taking a multitude of vitamins every day, like he did. Even though I didn't want to, I'd eventually given in to his wishes, because he could be quite charming and very persuasive. And sometimes it was simply easier to say yes than to argue back and forth. I didn't do well with too much drama in my life. Never had. I avoided conflict like the plague.

"You must be pretty antsy about this trip," he said, watching me walk to the sink.

"Not really," I lied, finishing up my second cup of coffee and rinsing out my favorite black and red mug in the sink.

"You could have fooled me. You tossed and turned most of the night."

"And how would you know?" I teased, staring at him. "Every time I looked over at you, you were knocked out, snoring like a bear in hibernation. You were oblivious to the world, including me," I said, handing him a carton of low-pulp orange juice from the refrigerator.

"That's what your good loving does to me," he said, reaching for me, pulling me into his arms, and caressing my butt through the thin rose-patterned silk robe I wore.

"Well, I still wish you could travel with me to North Carolina, to this small town outside of Raleigh."

"Baby, we've discussed this. I can't take that many days off from work right now. You'll be fine. I'll be there in spirit," he said, reaching for a glass in the cabinet.

"Work, work, work. Here we go again. It's always work. No, I couldn't possibly ask my executive-level boyfriend to miss a few precious days of work to accompany his woman to the funeral of one of her best friends. That would be totally selfish of me."

"Best friend? Huh? You hadn't seen her or spoken to her in over how many years did you say? Some friend."

"Ten," I said in a near whisper.

"Speak up. Ten years."

"That doesn't take away from the fact that we were once very close. I loved her."

"Whatever, Baldwin," he said, shaking his head, clearly irritated with me.

"What is that supposed to mean?" I asked.

"It means that as much as I care about you, I can't leave my commitments behind to tag along to babysit you with *your* group of ex-friends. I don't understand why you are so anxious to begin with, anyway."

I thought, *You wouldn't understand unless it makes money.* I didn't comment, just gave William a nasty look that let him know I wasn't pleased. Not in the least.

"Baldwin, the corporate world is very different from your nonprofit environment. You know that. You were once on the fast track and chose to give it up," William reminded me between gulps of the juice he had poured himself.

"Whatever."

"You're going to use my word against me now." He laughed. "Come here. Don't be like that," William said, reaching for me and easily pulling me back into his strong arms. "My baby's peeved at me."

I didn't resist too much.

"Baby, you know what I mean. Even though you are a director over at the United Way building, you can still afford to miss a few days," he said. "You don't have any pressing, urgent needs that demand your immediate attention."

"Like I said . . . whatever, William. Just forget I ever brought it up."

"Are you going to miss me?" he asked, kissing my neck. "I'm going to miss you."

I didn't comment. I pouted. That was what I did when I couldn't get my way.

"What? I can't hear you," he teased, tickling my sides until I smiled. "What did you say?"

"Yeah, I guess. Maybe a little," I said, trying my best not to crack another smile.

"You guess?" he asked, gently stroking my breasts through the opening of my thin floral silk robe, which he had given me as a Christmas present the previous year.

I moaned a little, tilted my head back. I slowly released the sash to my robe, and it fell open. With lust in his eyes, William continued to caress me as he parted my legs and inserted his middle finger deep inside after pulling my panties to the side. He knew my weak spots, but just as I was getting into a groove, he abruptly stopped.

"Why did you stop?" I asked, opening my eyes to take a peek at him.

"Why don't you give me something to take the edge off while you are away?"

"I took your edge off last night," I responded, irritated that he was no longer manually stimulating me.

"Give me a little more. You know what you do to me. I can never get enough of you, baby."

"I don't have time, sweetie," I said, glancing at the light blue kitchen clock that hung near the refrigerator. Time was flying by now.

"Come on. You have plenty of time," he replied, gently pushing my shoulders down toward the floor. "Your flight doesn't leave for another three hours. Take care of your man."

A few minutes later William had me exactly where he wanted. On my knees, with his chocolate dick in my mouth, as I gave him what he wanted . . . oral sex.

"Thank you, baby. I really needed that. You always give good head," he said as he helped me up. "I've got to get out of here, or I'm going to be late for work." He made a mad dash for the shower.

I was left standing with his come on my lips and with even more trepidation about my upcoming trip. Before she passed, my mother used to say, "Simply face your fears one step at a time. God never gives you more than you can handle." I silently prayed that God hadn't made a mistake this one time and didn't have me in over my head.

I'd find out soon enough.

Chapter 6

Baldwin

We don't have to change friends if we understand friends change.

I blankly stared straight ahead, looking at the back of the headrest of the seat directly in front of me. Even though I had a window seat, I couldn't get myself to glance out the window as the woodsy landscape of the area known as the Research Triangle Park of Raleigh-Durham came into full view. The short flight from Atlanta was coming to an end all too soon. I sighed and massaged by forehead, relaxing my frown lines.

"Ladies and gentlemen, we will be landing in approximately fifteen minutes, right on schedule. To prepare for landing, please place your seats in an upright position, hand any trash or discarded items to the flight attendants in the aisle, and remain seated with your seat belts on. The local time is twelve fifteen and the weather in the Raleigh-Durham area is a crisp fifty degrees. For those of you catching connecting flights, we wish you well in your continued travels and a representative will be posted at the gate to answer any questions you may have. As always, it has been a pleasure to serve you today."

I closed my eyes and took two deep, quick calming breaths. "One step at a time. One step." That was what

I kept telling myself, repeating it over and over again as I retrieved my small suitcase from the overhead compartment. That would be my mantra during my stay.

With my black carry-on and small black suitcase in tow, I exited the plane, slowly walked up the ramp to the gate, looked around, and spotted Bria immediately amid the small crowd of people, some standing and others casually seated near the gate. When she saw me, her pretty face instantly lit up like Christmas lights. She still looked much the same, maybe a few pounds heavier and a couple of dress sizes larger, but all in all she hadn't changed much.

In college, Bria was known for her long, slim legs, which went from here to eternity; her smooth tan, flawless complexion, and her shoulder-length, thick black hair. Today the long hair had been replaced with a chic symmetrical bob, and she was still as fashionable as a model prancing down a runway in Paris.

Bria and I reached each other in a few steps, hugged, and pulled away after a few moments and hugged again.

"Welcome back," she said with a huge genuine smile on her face as she took me in.

"I can't believe I'm here," I said, looking around in disbelief. "This was another lifetime," I declared, waving my hands around in awe.

"I remember when you told me that you'd never, ever set foot in this state again. At the time, I didn't think you were serious, but you kept your promise for a decade. I hope you realize you can't run from the past forever, though. Sooner or later it catches up with you."

"You look good. You haven't changed," I said to break the seriousness that was slowly creeping into the conversation already.

"Thank you. You do too, girl, and I'm feeling your short Halle Berry hairstyle. That's sharp. Wow, it's sooo good to see you!" she squealed, linking her arm through mine as best girlfriends do.

"You too," I said, and I really meant it. A smile crept onto my lips. With some people, no matter how much time passed, when you reconnected, it felt like you never missed a beat. Bria was one of those people.

"Do you have any bags that we need to pick up at the baggage claim?"

"Nope, this is it," I said, pointing to my two pieces. "I packed light."

"That you did. You wanted to guarantee you didn't stay too long," Bria kidded.

"Have the boys arrived yet?"

"Not yet. You're the first, so you and I can play catch-up as we wait for them. Christopher is driving in from Maryland, and Brenden said he would pick up a rental car once his flight lands from Chicago, because he didn't want to inconvenience anyone. I told him it would not be an inconvenience, but he insisted. Typical thoughtful Brenden. I've missed that man."

I nodded, not sure how to respond.

"But one thing is for sure."

"And what is that?" I asked.

"By tonight the group will be together again and the drinks will flow. That's a bet!" she said, winking conspiratorially.

"You haven't changed. Still crazy as ever," I said and picked up my pace to keep up with her long strides.

"And you know it."

The stroll to Bria's car in the underground parking deck, second level, was done mostly in silence, with a few instances of small talk thrown in for good measure. We talked about how nice the weather was going to be over the next few days, how Raleigh had changed from back in the day, and other topics. Finally we ran out of chitchat. Silence took its place and settled in. I guess we were both reflecting on better times.

"Let me pop the trunk, and then you can place your suitcases out of the way," Bria said, directing me to a black convertible that I could easily picture her zipping around town in. Carefree and fly.

"Okay. Thank you." We were back to being polite.

Once we had settled in the car, had clicked our seat belts, and had started slowly down the exit ramp, one of our songs from back in the day came on the radio. It was exactly the icebreaker that was needed at that moment in time.

"Uh-huh," Bria screamed, bopping her head and snapping her fingers to the beat. I hadn't forgotten how loud and crazy she could be.

"That's our song." I joined in, snapping my fingers, swaying my shoulders and head, and singing along. *"I like the way you work it. No diggity. I got to bag it up, bag it up."*

In less than five minutes, just like that, we had reverted back to our college days. We were singing, laughing, and enjoying true friendship, boundless energy and youth, and endless possibilities for the future facing us head-on. I recalled it all, all the fun we used to have. What happened?

"She's got class and style. Street knowledge, buy the pound."

All too soon the song ended, but the memories didn't.

"Wow. That takes me back," I said.

"Tell me about it. Remember the night after the big frat party when you, me, Rihanna, Christopher, and

Brenden drove out to the lake?" Bria asked. "We were so drunk, it was a damn shame. We were stumbling and falling all over the place. To be honest, I don't know how we made it out there."

"Through the grace of God."

"I guess it's going to be a little awkward being in the same space with Brenden after all these years, huh?" Bria asked, turning down the radio.

I shrugged. "He's moved on, and so have I."

"Everyone just knew the two of you would be married forever, with two-point-five babies and the white picket fence. Living the fairy-tale life."

"Well, we're not," I said in a near whisper. "He's with who he chose to be with."

"You think? I never liked that stank bitch," Bria stated with no shame.

I turned my body and faced the car window because I didn't want her to see the fresh pain I suddenly felt, which was clearly etched in my face.

"I'm sorry, Baldwin. I didn't mean to upset you. All that happened so long ago, and I just thought—"

"You didn't upset me. I'm fine," I lied, anxious to end the conversation.

"I didn't even ask, but tell me, are you married, divorced?" she asked, searching my finger for signs of a wedding band.

"No. Not yet, anyway. I've had a few relationships over the years, but I've never met the right one. Something was always missing. Plus, to be honest, I focused on my career and wasn't really interested in settling down. My career was my man. Then my priorities changed, and now I am in a committed two-year relationship."

"Good for you. Good for you, girl. We are not getting any younger."

"Speak for yourself," I said, laughing. "I may be getting older, but I'm definitely getting better and finally getting to know myself. Besides, who said thirty-two was old?"

"Who's thirty-two? I'm only thirty-one. Don't forget, I was one class behind you."

We laughed.

"What about you? What sexy man or men are in your life?"

"Believe me, you do not want to hear about my love life. You'd probably find it absolutely boring."

"No, I wouldn't, because as I recall, when it came to men, you were never boring. I've shared. Now it's your turn."

Bria paused.

"You haven't forgotten how we used to do it, have you? I share a truth and then you. Our version of Truth or Dare."

"I haven't forgotten. Looking back, those were the best days. We didn't realize how good we had it with no bills or major responsibilities."

"You can say that again," I said and sighed.

"And then we graduated, and the real world came calling. Like a damn telemarketer."

"I don't see a ring on your finger, either. Are you seeing anyone?" I asked, taking a quick glance at her ring finger.

Bria hesitated and started drumming her fingers nervously on the steering wheel. "My boyfriend and I have been together for four years now," she said in one long rushed breath, glancing at me from the corner of her eye.

"Wow. I guess you guys are pretty serious, huh?"

She smiled. "You could say that. I couldn't imagine life without him. We've been living together for about two years now."

"Oh my God. For real? Not you," I said, turning in my seat to face her, giving her my undivided attention.

"Yeah, it's true. Surprise, surprise," she replied, laughing. "I finally made a long-term commitment that lasted longer than a month."

"I can't believe you've settled down with one man, Bria. This is a new side of you I haven't seen before. When we were in college, you were . . . well . . ."

"Go on. You can say it. I know what I was. The word is promiscuous."

"You said it, not me," I said, laughing uncomfortably.

"You don't have to start sugarcoating anything with me, girl. In retrospect, I realize I made a lot of bad decisions and dumb choices."

"We all did," I volunteered. "Some of us more than others. It's all part of being young and dumb."

"For so many years I had been so unhappy, not really living. I was faking it, pretending to be happy. You know, laughing when I was supposed to. Being the life of the party because it was expected of me. Never meeting a stranger. Letting men use my body for their own satisfaction. Then I met and fell head over heels in love with a wonderful man named Terry. He changed my life, Baldwin."

The way she said her boyfriend's name, the way it literally flowed off her tongue, I sensed she loved him very much. Did I smile and did my eyes glaze over lovingly when I talked about William? I didn't think so. In fact, I knew that was the case.

"We have two dogs, Lucky and Chance, and a cat named Sponge Bob, after the cartoon character. We call them our babies. We are thinking about getting a parakeet."

I looked at Bria, beaming with love. She was simply glowing and couldn't stop smiling.

She glanced at me and saw me staring at her. "Listen to me going on and on like this. You didn't want to hear all that," she said, turning the radio up a bit.

"Don't stop on my behalf. I can tell you're very happy, and I'm happy for you."

Bria and I rode in silence for a while. I stared out the window and reacquainted myself with the passing landscape. Bria was right. A lot had changed. Finally, I couldn't control myself any longer. I had to know before curiosity killed me.

"How did he sound?" I quickly blurted out before I lost my nerve.

"Who?" she asked with a mischievous smile playing at the corners of her lips.

"How did Brenden sound?" I think that was the first time I had said his name out loud in years. It felt soothing, strange, and familiar all at the same time while rolling off my tongue.

"He sounded great, real mature and all about business. You know, same ole Brenden. He was just as shocked as everyone else to find out about Rihanna passing."

"I'm sure. I still can't believe it," I said. "It's almost like the reality of it hasn't set in yet."

"We didn't talk long, but he did ask if I had talked to you."

I couldn't trust myself to say anything at that revelation. For some unknown reason, I was secretly happy and pissed that he had asked about me.

Bria continued. "Brenden said he was looking forward to seeing you and having the opportunity to talk if you decided to come. He wasn't so sure you would come, knowing he'd be here."

"Oh, did he? Isn't he married? Married to 'I'll sleep with anyone' Malia Collins?"

Bria frowned. "He was, but who knows? Many of our classmates have married, divorced, and remarried by now. I heard that Herman Foster has been married and divorced at least three times now."

"Bad breath, 'you can smell him coming a mile away' Herman Foster?"

"'I'll fuck anything with a vagina and I take a bath every three days' Herman Foster. That would be the one." Bria laughed. "But you'll have plenty of time to find out about Brenden, won't you?"

I thought that I would, and that was what was worrying me.

The remainder of the drive was done in silence, with just the radio playing music, which took me back to when love was real and true and good, before it all went so wrong and innocence was destroyed and lost, never to be found again.

"I never knew till I looked in your eyes. I was incomplete till the day you walked into my life. And I never knew that my heart could feel so precious and pure, one love so real," sang Eric Benet on the radio.

No, we couldn't run from our past forever. It did catch up with you sooner or later. In fact, Bria was driving us directly to it.

Chapter 7

Baldwin

I've learned that even when you think you have no more to give, when a friend cries out to you, you will find the strength to help.

Thirty, maybe forty minutes later, Bria and I pulled onto a winding, secluded secondary road and drove about a mile back through a dense cluster of pine trees on each side whose branches met in the middle, creating a canopy of nature.

"Are you sure this is the right way? Did we make a wrong turn?" I asked, squirming in my seat.

"This is what the navigation system says is the right direction, and Mrs. Brown said the house was back off the main road, in a rural setting."

"Yeah, this is definitely pretty rural I'd say. We haven't even seen many homes."

"I think we are almost there," Bria said, studying the navigation system screen.

"I hope so. If we don't see the house soon, let's turn around. Okay? These navigation systems will have you out in the middle of nowhere. I've heard stories of people driving into cemeteries, getting stuck on mountaintops, or even driving into rivers."

"Driving into rivers? I see you are still a big scaredycat." Bria laughed. "Man up, girl. You're in good hands with me."

Bria and I drove for approximately another half mile. Sure enough, sitting off by itself at a turn in the road was Rihanna's house. We slowed down to a crawl as we approached. Even from the outside I could feel Rihanna's spirit reaching out to greet us. Embracing us. Welcoming us.

The small house was modest, but with a lot of character, just like our dear departed friend. The house was white with black shutters, a bright red door, and a white picket fence. I noticed a small vegetable garden positioned near the well-manicured backyard and also a red birdhouse, perched on a small post upon a miniature hill. Squirrels pranced around in the treetops, as if announcing and rejoicing in our sudden arrival.

Pulling up into the driveway and turning off the engine, Bria said, "Number two-zero-five. Looks like this is it."

I felt a heavy lump form in the back of my throat, and I could only nod my head. I couldn't trust myself to speak. Neither of us was making any effort to get out of the car and walk the short distance to the front door.

"This has Rihanna written all over it. I can easily picture her living here, growing her organic vegetables and sitting on the front porch, in one of those white rocking chairs in the evenings, with a romance book in hand. She loved those romance novels," I managed to say, staring straight ahead. "She believed in the black knight in shining armor."

I glanced over at Bria and noticed her eyes watering up, her tears threatening to spring forth and spill, as mine ran down my cheeks in streams.

"I can't believe she's gone, Baldwin. Life is short, but Rihanna left too soon. All the good ones leave too soon. Why? It doesn't seem fair. She never hurt a fly."

"I feel so sorry for Mrs. Brown. I wonder how she's holding up. Rihanna was her only child, and we both know how much she doted on her," I said in a shaky, trembling voice that I didn't recognize as my own.

"I could have been a better friend. We lived right here in the same state, only two hours from one another, but the best I could do was a phone call every few years or a generic Christmas card in the mail during the holidays."

"Don't beat up on yourself," I said. "Obviously, she valued your friendship, or you wouldn't have been left in her will. So you made a difference in her life."

"What happened to us, Baldwin? We were like sisters, and Brenden and Christopher were like the brothers I never had," Bria said, turning in the driver's seat to face me.

"One word. Life. Life happened. And sometimes there are words spoken and events that unfold that can never be taken back. They change the dynamics of a friendship forever."

"It just all seems so unfair. We weren't supposed to end up like this, losing touch with one another, but I'm happy you are here, because I couldn't handle this by myself." She smiled lovingly. "Are you ready to do this?" she asked, opening her car door.

"Ready as I will ever be," I said, opening my door and stepping out. "We can do anything together. There is strength in numbers."

"Mrs. Brown said she'd leave the house key under the welcome mat for us to let ourselves in and she'd drop by later to check on us."

"That's sweet. I always did like Rihanna's mom. Whenever she'd come to campus to visit, she'd always bring those huge home-cooked meals wrapped up in thick foil, enough for all of us. And remember those care packages she would send Rihanna once a month? I think we enjoyed their arrival just as much as Rihanna did."

Bria nodded.

"Mrs. Brown used to call herself our second mom, and I appreciated that, since my mom was all the way in Georgia," I said. "Her chocolate cake was to die for, too delicious to put into words. Her cakes made you want to slap your momma. My mouth is watering up thinking of it."

Bria opened the trunk. We retrieved our suitcases and made our way up the narrow walkway to the cozy front porch. Sure enough, directly under a mat that said FRIENDS ARE ALWAYS WELCOME, we found the house key. I silently wondered if that truly applied to us anymore. Ten years was a lifetime.

Chapter 8

Baldwin

With Bria leading the way, she and I entered the house cautiously, as if at any moment Rihanna would jump out from some hidden spot and scream, "Surprise!" She would explain how this was all an elaborate plan to get us back together again. She didn't really die from breast cancer.

However, that didn't happen. Life wasn't that kind. Stepping through the front door, our bags in tow, was like spying on Rihanna's life—life after college, life after our friendship, life in the real world. The place was decorated in bright, bold, vibrant colors, much like the person Rihanna was.

"I don't know about you, girl, but I feel like we are flies on the wall, peeking into Rihanna's life," Bria volunteered, looking around hesitantly as we inched our way deeper into the cozy sunken living room.

We set our luggage down and continued to explore. We walked with our shoulders touching from room to room, from the first floor to upstairs, picking up photos, seeing the smiling, always smiling face of our dear departed friend.

"I don't think I can do this," I cried in between sniffles.

"Don't you dare start crying, because if you do, I will," Bria explained. "I can't believe she had a will. Who has a will at our age? At thirty-two?"

"Someone who has a terminal illness and thinks about death and dying. A responsible, reliable person like Rihanna. She always was more wise and mature than any of us ever were."

"Look, Baldwin," Bria stated, picking up a five-by-seven photo in a silver and gold decorative frame that was sitting on a hallway table.

"Oh my God, that's us. Now, that takes me back." I giggled.

"Where did we take this?" Bria asked, studying the picture intensely, deep in thought.

"I think that was the night we decided to fill up the gas tank and ride until we came to the ocean. We didn't care that we had about thirty dollars total to our name." I laughed. "Look at us. We look so happy and young and adventurous."

"We do, don't we? Hell, we were. Those were the days. College is some of the best days of your life. Look at that shirt Christopher was wearing." Bria chuckled, placing the photo carefully back on the table. "I can't wait to see him."

"What are you talking about? That was stylish back in the day. Remember, he was one of the best dressed men on campus."

"Look at him. He just knew he was a playa playa. Sexy motherfucker."

I chuckled because I knew I couldn't disagree. He definitely had a way with the ladies. I think he even had a few men with secret crushes on him.

Bria and I continued exploring, taking in the woman Rihanna became after college. We came to a room that looked like the master bedroom. We peeked in but couldn't go in, not yet, anyway. Rihanna's aura poured from the walls like a sparkling waterfall.

***

An hour later, Bria and I were unpacked and lazily sitting at the tiny kitchen table. I was drinking instant coffee, and Bria was sipping on Sam's Club bottled water, which we had found after some digging around in the cabinets. Minus the master bedroom, there were three smaller bedrooms upstairs. Bria and I decided to share one, much like we had as college roommates. I didn't think any one of us wanted to be alone. That left Brenden and Christopher with their own room.

Bria checked her watch. "The rest of the group should be arriving soon. I guess we could cook and have dinner waiting for them. I'm sure they would love a hot meal."

"Since when did you become domesticated?" I laughed. "I remember when you lived for days off of hamburgers, Domino's pizza, ramen noodles, and Big Chik and didn't gain a damn pound. For a minute, I thought you were bulimic or anorexic."

"Well, people change." She smiled.

"That we do. Thank God."

"Did you really think I had an eating disorder?"

"Hell no, not for long. I soon found out you adored two things. Food and sex."

"We all had our vices. Mine just happened to be eating and fucking, not necessarily in that order. In fact, it worked out better if I was eaten and then fucked."

I placed my hand over my mouth in mock shock over her abrasiveness.

"What? What did I say?"

"Nothing, Bria. Better to have those two vices than for it to be an actual person," I shared.

I walked the few steps over to the refrigerator and pulled open the door again. The refrigerator looked like it had been recently cleaned out, because it was pretty much bare. There was half a pint of milk, a package of wheat bread, and some orange juice, but nothing to cook a meal for four. I had lucked out in finding instant coffee in one of the cabinets in the far corner.

"It looks like we are going to have to make a run to the grocery store," I said.

"And the liquor store for beer and wine."

"If you say so," I agreed.

"Let's do this. You stay here and wait on the rest of the group, and I'll pick up some groceries and drinks," Bria offered.

"Are you sure? We could both go and knock it out a lot quicker. It shouldn't take that long."

"I don't want Brenden and Christopher to arrive and not find anyone here, or what if they need directions? They may try to call the house."

I nodded in agreement. "True. Okay. I'll stay and be the official greeter."

"I won't take long, and you'll be okay. Rihanna is not going to jump out and bite you."

"Ha. Ha. Ha." I wondered why she was the second person in the past few days who had told me I'd be okay.

Bria and I scribbled a quick grocery list, mostly staple items that would get us through the next few days. I made sure she added my favorite brand of gourmet coffee to the list, Oreo cookies for Christopher, and Doritos for Brenden. I couldn't believe I remembered they loved those snacks. Bria grabbed her fashionable purse and keys and left for the grocery store that we had seen while driving in.

With Bria gone, I didn't know what to do with myself. I felt strange being in Rihanna's home alone; I kept looking over my shoulder, expecting to see someone. I flipped distractedly through a few decorating, home and garden, and cooking magazines lying on the coffee table.

I turned the TV on, and just as quickly turned it back off. The noise was too much, and I needed time to think.

One step at a time. One step at a time.

Finally, I walked upstairs and picked the photo back up. I stared at myself in the picture. Brenden had his arms wrapped tightly around my waist, like he'd never let go. But he did. He did let go.

I had the biggest, happiest smile on my face. Pure bliss. All was fine in my world, and you couldn't tell me any different. How immature of me to think things would never change. At that moment, I think I was the happiest I had ever been. I thought long and hard and hard and long as to when I lost that joy. The better question was, would I ever find it again?

The ringing doorbell interrupted my reflection and made me jump as chimes sounded throughout the house. I sprinted down the stairs two at a time.

"Bria, what did you forget?" I asked, flinging the door wide open without bothering to see who was on the other side.

My past awaited me.

Chapter 9

Baldwin

"Well, look what the wind blew in," Christopher said, halfway picking me up off the floor in a big bear hug.

"Christopher! Wow! You look great, man. Come in," I said, stepping back after he released me so he could enter. "Wow! Look at you! I can't believe you're here."

"So do you, baby girl. So do you," he said, looking me up and down in an appreciative manner. "I see baby girl finally got back." He laughed, checking out my rear end as he circled around me, pretending to look me over.

"Don't start with me, Christopher," I said, playfully punching his arm. "Stop being mannish."

"Ouch. What did I do?" he asked, massaging the top portion of his left arm.

"Boy, stop acting. I didn't hit you that hard." I laughed.

"I'm just admiring how you finally filled out. You're looking good, but then you always did, Baldwin."

Back in the day, Christopher was a ladies' man on campus. Even if he weren't over six foot tall, light-skinned, well built, and handsome, his personality would still win you over all by itself. He was fun to be around and was always doing something crazy. He was one of those people who you couldn't dare to do anything . . . because he would do it.

One weekend when Bria and I were bored out of our minds, Christopher dropped by and we dared him to run buck naked from one end of our dorm hallway to the next. What did he do? You guessed it. He did it. Christopher was in a popular fraternity, ran track and had broken records, and was the president of the Black Student Organization.

"Where's your partner in crime? Has she not gotten here yet?" he asked, leaving his bag in the foyer, taking a seat on the sofa, and making himself comfortable. I closed the door and walked in behind him.

"Bria went to the store to pick up groceries, but she'll be back soon and can't wait to see you. That's all she has been talking about."

"Where's your man?" he asked, looking amused.

"Back home in Georgia."

"Baldwin, you know who I'm talking about."

"If you're referring to Brenden, he hasn't arrived yet, and it's been a very long time since he was my man."

"Okay, don't go getting an attitude on me. I'm just playing with you, baby girl."

I shrugged my shoulders and sat down across from him on the microfiber love seat, tucking my foot underneath me.

"How are you holding up?" I asked.

"I still can't believe our girl is gone. What about you?"

"Same here. I'm hanging in there, and I keep thinking I'll wake up and this will all be a very bad dream," I said.

"To this day, I don't think I've met a woman as sweet and gentle as she was," he said, looking away, not meeting my eyes.

"Rihanna was beautiful inside and out, but sometimes she would let her weight issues get her down, and I hated that," I said. "If a man couldn't see past the weight, then it was his loss."

"It's a shame she never found someone to make her happy, to treat her the way she deserved to be treated," Christopher said, staring off into space.

"Bria and I always thought she had a secret crush on you, but then again everyone had a crush on you. Everyone loved Christopher. You broke a lot of hearts on campus, boy," I said, kidding with him.

"Not everyone. You didn't."

"Didn't what?"

"You never had a crush on me."

"Huh, I knew how trifling your ass was. Plus, I have never gone for the pretty boy type."

"That was many years ago. I was a young man, sowing my seed."

"Sowing you did, and you did it very well, all over campus."

"I did it very well, huh?" He grinned.

"I heard the stories," I said, turning away. Christopher could always make me blush, and he got great joy out of doing so.

"Well, now I'm a grown-ass man who's trying his best to be in a committed relationship with a beautiful woman back home."

"There's that word again."

"What word?"

"*Committed.* It seems everyone is mature and in a serious relationship. First Bria, now you. There must be something in the air that I didn't breathe in."

"I'm trying my damnedest. Who's managed to slow Wild Child down?"

I laughed. "I'll let her tell you herself. I had forgotten that was what you used to call her. Wild Child. It's amazing what we remember and what we choose to forget over the years." I looked up from my spot on the love seat to find Christopher boldly staring at me. "What?" I asked, feeling a bit self-conscious under his steady gaze.

"Nothing. I'm just thinking that you haven't changed much."

"I hope that's a good thing."

"No, don't get me wrong. It is a very good thing."

I smiled and turned away to break his scrutiny.

"You always were one of the most levelheaded of all of us," he said.

"I won't deny that."

"It's hard to believe ten years have flown by so quickly. You look up, and they are ghost, just like that. I've missed you in my life, Baldwin. I really have."

We were silent. Words unspoken. Deeds known.

"Hey, you're not off the hook, by the way. What's up with you in the relationship department?" he asked, breaking the moment of awkwardness that had permeated the space we shared.

"I am dating someone, and we've been together for two years now."

"Do you live together?"

"Absolutely not. He stays over occasionally."

"And?"

"And what?" I asked.

"Why all the secrecy? What's up with your man? Tell me about him."

"I'm sure you don't want to hear all the boring details of my love life."

He laughed. "You're right. I was just being nice."

"What?"

"I'm kidding, Baldwin. You know I love you like a sister. I always had your best interest in mind. Just tell me, is this mystery man treating you right?"

I didn't answer right away. I found myself getting more and more uncomfortable with his line of questioning.

"I sense a hesitation. What's up with that?" he questioned, suddenly looking serious.

"His name is William, and yes, most of the time he treats me well. We have our ups and downs like most relationships."

"Well, we can't have that. One hundred percent of the time or nothing. You should have listened to me years ago, when I told you Brenden was the one, baby girl."

Holding up my hand, I said, "Don't start bringing up the past, Christopher."

"Hear me out first. You don't even know what I'm going to say."

"I'm serious. That's water under the bridge. Deep, murky water. Don't wade there."

"What are you so afraid of, Baldwin? Like you said, that was eons ago, but I know for a fact that man loved you. One of the last serious conversations he and I had was about you," he said, leaning forward. "It was late Friday night. I stumbled into the apartment we shared, half drunk as usual and—"

"I really don't want to hear this."

"And Brenden—"

"Stop! I'm not listening," I shouted, getting up off the sofa.

"Okay, I know when my advice is unwanted and—"

Just at that time, the front door burst wide open, like someone had kicked it in. "Christopher! Come here, dude, and give me some love," Bria screamed, running over, arms wide open, and literally jumped on him as he stood. "I saw your car outside with the out-of-state Maryland license plate."

"Still our very own wild child. What's good?" he asked, holding her back to look her over with a big smile on his handsome face.

"Oh, damn! I had forgotten that," she said, looking at me. "You're still handsome as ever, Christopher. Are you still getting all the pussy you can handle?"

"I see you still have that filthy mouth too. But what can I say? I'm irresistible to women. Most, anyway," Christopher teased, glancing my way.

"Baldwin, remember when he used to trick those stupid freshman girls into giving him blow jobs? Told them it was part of initiation into becoming a little sister of his fraternity, and they'd fall for it every time."

I reclined on the sofa, taking it all in, simply watching the exchange. Old memories and feelings rushed back and hit me smack in the face. In that room, at that moment, I remembered I loved those people. My heart told me so.

"Bria, close the door. It's chilly outside," I said. "You're letting out all the heat."

"Okay, but y'all need to help me bring those groceries in. Ain't no damn maids up in here," she teased.

"Okay, give me a minute. You too, Christopher. You heard her. Ain't no maids in this joint," I joked.

We were easily falling back into our previous roles, and the shoes fit. They felt comfortable, fuzzy, and warm.

Just as I got up to grab my peacoat and multicolored knit scarf, which I had placed in the coat closet, the door quietly swung open, and in the doorway stood Brenden.

A blast from my past.

Chapter 10

Baldwin

I believe that maturity has more to do with what types of experiences you've had and what you've learned from them and less to do with how many birthdays you've created.

This was the moment, in the back of my mind, barely scratching the surface, the moment that I had fantasized about for almost ten years. I had waited years to come face-to-face with Brenden again, to look into his handsome face and figure out why we had ceased to exist, why he had stopped loving me, seemingly overnight.

As corny as it might sound, time stood absolutely still, or at least it appeared to.

Movement appeared to slow down at an exaggerated speed, and the noise level was at a near whisper, because I couldn't hear over the frantic beating of my heart as blood rushed to my ears. I was glued to my spot near the front door, like someone had spread Krazy Glue on the bottom of my shoes, as everyone exchanged eager greetings. I took it all in with utter awe . . . like I was having an out-of-body experience. I was there in body, but I really wasn't. Slowly, finally, the fuzziness cleared from my brain and I could think. I remembered my name.

"Brenden! You made it!" Bria screamed, jumping all over him, much the same as she had done to Christopher upon his arrival.

Brenden smiled. "What's up, Bria? It's good to see you."

They embraced, and Brenden kissed her lightly on the cheek. Since Bria was all over him, I still hadn't gotten a really good look at him yet, just his profile. However, his deep, soulful voice took me back and gave me tiny goose bumps, which raced and zigzagged up and down my arms. I tried to sneak a peek around Bria without him noticing.

Next was Christopher's turn. He stood in front of Brenden, and they embraced as men do, shaking hands and doing the shoulder bump. Unspoken words and experiences were exchanged through their eyes, then disappeared just as quickly. The past was the past, and it had its place in the recesses of our hearts.

"What's up, my man?" Christopher asked. "It's been a long time."

"Yeah, too long. I had to come back and say my farewell. Talking about life not being fair, Rihanna definitely got the short end of the deal," Brenden said.

"I know it," Christopher agreed, shaking his head.

Then, like the parting of the Red Sea, all eyes turned and focused my way. For a split second, I felt like fleeing up the stairs and out of sight, escaping the unwanted spotlight. I got my first full, unobstructed view of Brenden, and my breath literally caught in my throat. If it was possible to experience overwhelming emotion from just the sight of another human being, then that was exactly what happened. When our eyes locked on each other, I felt my heart lurch forward. Until that moment I had never realized how much I missed him.

"Hello, Baldwin," he said quietly, staring almost through me with those bright light green eyes, which always looked like they could see right to my very soul, exposing my thoughts and feelings.

"Hey. How are you?" I asked, taking a step backward, retreating from his unrelenting glare. I couldn't trust myself to say more or be any closer to him.

"I've been better."

Christopher and Bria were watching the exchange as if they were spectators at a tennis match. Their heads moved back and forth, back and forth, from one to the other of us as we spoke. Amusement clearly shone in their sparkling eyes.

Brenden stepped toward me, and I slid back again, taking another step out of his reach. I had forgotten how tall he was as I looked up at him. He was lean, yet firm and muscular. He now wore his hair in a low cut style, and there were small signs of maturity around his eyes, but other than that, he was the same handsome man I had fallen in love with before he walked out and stomped all over my heart like it was nothing, like I didn't matter. Like I was replaceable. And I guess I was. It was at that precise moment, I realized I had never forgiven him for that. I resented him for making me feel unworthy of his love. All my anger rushed to the surface, simmering like a stew before boiling over.

"Can I get a hug?" he asked with outstretched arms.

I glared back at him. "I don't know. Can you?" I asked with much attitude.

"Ahhh, come on, Baldwin. Show the man some love," Bria chimed in. "You haven't seen him in years."

I turned and glared at her, like she had said the most ludicrous statement ever, rolled my eyes, and suddenly realized how stupid I was acting. All over something that was irrelevant now. All over something that happened years ago. All over a boy who was now a man. I was no longer twenty-one years old and deliciously in love for the first time.

We had all moved on with our lives. We were mature adults now who were living in the real, harsh world. Brenden simply wasn't important, wasn't even a part of my life. I could deal with him for the next few days. William was my man, and he was at home, waiting for me.

"Give her a hug, man," Christopher said in amusement. "Baldwin is waiting for you to make the first move. You know how she is, all reserved and ladylike."

Brenden looked to me for confirmation, and I stepped forward with my arms stretched wide open, a half smile glued to my lips. When he pulled me near and wrapped his muscular arms around my back, I relished his embrace. I closed my eyes, took in his masculine scent, and remembered. Remembered how much I once loved this man, remembered how he was the first man to make me feel like a woman, not like a little girl. I remembered it all, vividly.

Brenden whispered softly, "I've missed you, Baldwin. I've missed you so much. I never forgot you. You even showed up in my dreams at night."

I abruptly pulled away, like I had been scorched by sparks from a blazing fire. His simple words ignited a fire in me, a passion that I hadn't felt since we went our separate ways. This man was dangerous, and I was determined to keep my distance for the next few days.

Chapter 11

Baldwin

Sometimes when I'm angry, I have the right to be angry, but that doesn't give me the right to be cruel.

For the remainder of the evening, I avoided Brenden like a bad, itchy, inflamed rash. I made sure I was never alone with him in the living room, and I couldn't quite get myself to look directly at him, because I knew my eyes would say it all and betray me. No words would be necessary.

Even though I didn't like the reason for our reunion, I intended to prove to myself and to Brenden, once and for all, that he no longer meant anything to me. He was just a man I used to love, gave myself to . . . in another time and place. I yearned for Brenden to witness the strong, independent woman I had become without him. I wanted him to see and know I didn't need him. I didn't miss him. I was doing just fine without him. My life didn't stop because he rejected me.

It was around 7:00 P.M. or so, and Bria and I were finishing up in the kitchen. She and I had fried crispy chicken and had cooked green beans and macaroni and cheese. Bria had even fixed some sweet iced tea. We were sitting comfortably at the kitchen table, waiting patiently on the last few pieces of chicken to fry. The guys had gotten unpacked and settled upstairs, and they were in the living room, in front of the TV, catching up with one another, with sprinkles of conversation filtering our way.

"Girl, what do you think?" Bria inquired, nodding toward the living room. "Brenden is still as handsome as ever. He's like a fine wine, gets better with age."

"He's okay," I said, getting up, opening and closing kitchen drawers to find silverware to set the table. I felt a desire to keep busy.

"Okay? Yeah, right. I saw the way he pulled you into his arms and you simply melted. Where there's heat, there's fire."

I didn't comment one way or the other, just continued to arrange the place settings I had found.

"Can you honestly stand there and say you didn't feel anything for him? Love? Lust? Damn, something?" Bria asked.

"I can and I will, Bria. I didn't feel anything. Not a damn thing." I smirked, looking directly at her.

"Uh-huh," she said, looking like she didn't believe a word I had spoken. "You don't have the desire to fuck him for old time's sake?" she asked, turning over the last piece of a golden fried chicken, a leg, which hissed and sizzled in Crisco oil.

"No, I don't. I have a man back home who keeps me satisfied in the bedroom. Thank you very much."

"And I understand that, but it would be normal for old feelings to resurface, seeing as how—"

"I don't know why you and Christopher keep trying to throw me and Brenden together. It's simply not going to happen. Now or ever. I know you guys mean well, but forget it. Stay out of my business. It's not happening. First of all, I don't do married men, and besides I'm in a relationship."

"So old feelings didn't rush to the surface?"

"Bria!" I screamed. "Did you hear anything I just said? No."

"If you keep repeating that enough, sooner or later you'll believe it," she said, shaking her head.

"What do you want me to say?"

"The truth."

As I wrung my hands, we stared each other down for a few seconds before I dropped my glare. Bria hadn't changed; she had always wanted to be right and have the last word.

"Hey, ladies. Somebody's cell is going off in the living room, and it ain't ours," Christopher said, strolling into the kitchen. "Hmmm, something smells good up in here."

"We'll talk about this later," Bria whispered. "We are not finished by a long shot."

I shrugged and walked around her. I hurried into the living room after hearing my familiar ring tone and found my purse on the floor near the love seat, directly across from where Brenden was sprawled out. I made every effort not to look at him as I retrieved my Black-Berry.

"Hello," I said, sitting at the far end of the sofa, as far away from him as possible. I smiled. "Hey, sweetie. I miss you too," I cooed seductively.

At the mention of the word *sweetie,* out of the corner of my eye, I noticed Brenden glance in my direction.

"Yes. I'm here safe and sound. My flight was fine, and Bria was waiting for me at the airport as promised."

I laughed at something William said, and when I looked over at Brenden, he was not even trying to hide the fact that he was all up in my personal conversation. He wasn't even faking like he was watching TV anymore.

"The group is about to sit down to dinner now. . . . Sure. . . . I will. . . . I wish you were here too, and I miss you already."

I glanced up again, and Brenden hadn't moved. Our eyes met, and I instantly averted mine. I vaguely heard Christopher in the kitchen, chatting and kidding around with Bria.

"You are bad." I giggled. "I'm not going to say that over the phone. No, they might hear me," I whispered. "Goodnight, sweetie." I pressed the end button and disconnected the call just as Bria announced dinner was served.

Brenden stood up just as I was easing past him. "Was that your man?" he asked.

"Something like that," I said, barely looking back.

He scowled. "Either he is or he isn't. Which is it?"

I stopped in mid-step. "Why does it matter to you?"

"I only asked a simple question, Baldwin. I see you haven't changed much. You still overanalyze every-thing people say to you."

"Your only concern should be your wifey, and that certainly isn't me," I said between clenched teeth as I walked into the kitchen with Brenden on my heels.

I had a feeling that this was going to be a very long next few days. For now, my one desire was to make it through dinner without going off on him again.

Chapter 12

Baldwin

*My best friends and I can do anything or nothing
and have the best time.*

During the heated exchange between Brenden and
me, Bria had taken it upon herself to create a nice, cozy
table. The rectangular wooden table was set with pale
blue paisley-patterned china plates, silver-plated flat-
ware, and crystal long-stemmed wineglasses, and as an
added bonus, the lights were dimmed as we dined by
candlelight.

"Can you guys believe we are back together after all
these years?" Bria asked, looking at each of us from her
seat at the head of the table. Christopher faced her on
the opposite end, which left me to her right and Brenden to her left, with him and me facing one another.

"Too bad it's under these circumstances," I said wea-
rily. "It still hasn't sunk in that Rihanna is not coming
back. This is all so surreal."

Silence followed as we were momentarily lost in
thought.

"You guys haven't changed a bit," Bria said, smiling
as she broke the silence.

"You sure have, Wild Child. You never could throw
down like this back in the day. In fact, I don't recall
ever seeing you cook anything, except maybe boiling

some water for some ramen noodles. Rihanna was always the cook," Christopher said in between hearty bites of a crispy Southern fried chicken leg cooked to perfection.

Brenden chuckled as he watched him tear into his food like it was his last meal.

"What?" Christopher asked, looking up from his over-flowing plate.

"You haven't changed, either, because you can still eat a person out of house and home," I said and chuck-led. "Rihanna always cooked extra for you and your greedy self."

Christopher took another extra-big bite and winked at me. "I can't help it if I have a healthy appetite, baby girl."

"What's going on with everybody? What did life hold for each of you after graduation?" Brenden questioned as his eyes hungrily lingered on me. "It never crossed my mind that it might not turn out the way I thought it would."

I averted my eyes as I took a sip of wine.

"I can go first. I'm a buyer for the juniors department of a major department store chain," Bria volunteered, lifting her glass of wine for a sip as well.

"Good for you. That sounds exciting," I said. "I can see you doing that, Bria, and I'm sure you're excellent at it. You always were the creative fashionista type. You could make a ripped T-shirt and men's boxers look good."

"Sometimes it is very exciting and thrilling . . . ten percent of the time," Bria revealed. "I get to travel to New York, attend fashion shows, and I've even gone to Paris. Most people only see the glamorous side of the industry, but my job entails a lot of hard work and long hours. At the end of the day, though, I can honestly say

I love my job. I'm eager to roll out of bed each morning."

"I can second that, Bria. I know exactly how you feel. I'm a sports agent for one of the top ten firms. My job comes with a fair amount of travel and, of course, recruiting some of the top talent in the country," Christopher said. "But I love what I do and wouldn't trade it for anything in the world. Making talented young guys into overnight millionaires, instantly changing their lives and their families' and making their dreams come true, is amazing and very fulfilling."

"That's very cool, Christopher. You were able to combine your love of sports, your gift of gab, and salesmanship into a lucrative career," Brenden said, looking impressed.

"Well, I'm afraid my job isn't quite as exciting as the two of yours," I said, looking at Bria and Christopher, ignoring Brenden. "A few years ago I was on the fast track in corporate America. The money was excellent, but I wasn't fulfilled. Something was missing. So I gave it all up, simply walked away, and never looked back. Now I work for a nonprofit organization, and I'm giving back to the community," I said. "At the end of the day, I feel like I'm making a difference in the world, and I can sleep better at night."

"Better you than me, girlfriend. Nonprofits are notorious for low pay and lack of resources. How's that working out?" Bria asked, taking a big gulp of wine.

"I'm not going to lie. I admit it was hard at first. I remember the first time I saw my paycheck, I almost screamed out loud, but I adjusted. There is something special in knowing I've made a positive impact on someone's life. That puts a smile on my face that is priceless. Money isn't everything, Bria."

"The hell it ain't," she said jokingly.

Christopher looked over at me and smiled as I took a few bites of creamy macaroni and green beans.

"It's a small world, Baldwin," said Brenden. "I work for a nonprofit in Chicago, and I understand exactly what you mean about making a difference. There is no feeling like it. I get to make an impact on the lives of young boys and girls, our future leaders, each and every day at the Boys & Girls Club of America."

Brenden caught my eye again, and I reached for my wineglass, not commenting.

"I'm not surprised, Brenden, that you chose that career path. You were always the do-gooder of the bunch," Christopher said. "You were going to change the world all by yourself."

"Where was Rihanna working before she passed?" I asked.

"She owned and managed a small children's clothing boutique in town," Bria interjected.

"I can see her doing that because she really loved kids," I said, picking up some green beans with my fork. "That was right up her alley. Remember when she worked at the on-campus day care and would talk for hours about the kids who attended? Many of them were from low-income families."

Everyone nodded in agreement, the mood changing to one of sadness at the mention of Rihanna's name.

"This calls for a toast," Christopher stated, raising his glass. We lifted our wineglasses in turn. "Here's to renewed friendships and the ties that bind."

"Cheers! Cheers! Cheers!" we chanted in unison, clicking glassware.

"Who's married, in a serious relationship, or single?" Bria asked, purposely not looking at me, because she knew I sensed the direction this was headed in.

The alcohol was definitely making everyone loosen up, as the conversation flowed freely, just like old times.

"I'm trying my best to be in a committed, faithful relationship," Christopher revealed. "But it's hard with all the women I meet on the road who want to get a taste." He laughed, reaching across the table and pumping fists with Brenden.

"What? Not playa, playa over here?" Bria laughed. "I know you, of all people, aren't complaining about all the women trying to throw pussy your way."

"I couldn't believe it at first my damn self, but I've met *the one*, the future Mrs. Christopher Bivins. All the others dim in comparison."

"Not the one. Well, we definitely have to meet her. The one woman who can settle your ass down has got to be extra special," I kidded.

"Personally, I'll believe it when I see it. I've never heard of a zebra changing its stripes," Bria said jokingly. "But I have heard that a dog will be a dog. Ruff, ruff."

Brenden had gotten up and had skillfully opened the bottle of red wine sitting on the counter and was refilling everyone's near empty glasses. As the wine flowed, guards were let down and old friendships were renewed.

"What about you, Brenden?" Bria asked. "As I recall, you tied the knot shortly after graduation, so you should be a pro at this marriage thing by now."

He sighed. "Apparently not. We're separated. Have been for a few months now." He glanced my way, as if I cared. "Marriage is more work than I ever imagined, especially when you're in it for all the wrong reasons."

Bria slyly kicked me under the table, and I gave her the evil eye. I felt Brenden still staring my way, but I refused to acknowledge him in any form or fashion.

He continued. "I probably should have left years ago, but I tried to hang in there for my son's sake. Now I realize he'd be happier with two parents, under two separate roofs, who aren't at each other's throats all the time. He simply needs to know he is loved."

"Ahhh, Brenden's a daddy," Bria said, slightly slurring her words as she reached for another refill from the wine bottle that was sitting on the table. "And I agree one hundred percent. Children just need to feel loved."

"My son, Jordan, I can honestly say he's the love of my life," Brenden gushed with a huge smile that spoke to that absolute truth. His eyes literally twinkled when he spoke of his offspring.

"That's great, man," Christopher said. "Real cool. Jordan's a lucky kid."

"What's the deal with you, baby girl?" Christopher asked. "Earlier you were all secretive and shit."

"I was not, Christopher. Why are you lying?" I asked, feeling a light buzz.

"You were. You weren't even going to tell me dude's name until I pressed."

"Stop playing. I told you his name, and I've been dating William for almost two years now," I said as I felt the cool liquid start to warm me up from inside out.

"Is it serious? I mean, after two years, that's an investment in my book," Bria said, reclining in her chair, eyes slightly glazed over.

"If you mean, are we planning a wedding? No." I shook my head.

"Why not?" she asked, stretching her long legs into Brenden's lap. He began to massage her shoeless right foot. "Hmmm, you always were the best foot massager, Brenden. Why not, Baldwin? What were you saying?" She looked at me through hooded eyelids.

"I don't know. We just never talked about it, because we're content with the way things are. We don't need a marriage license to prove anything. But enough about me, Bria. Tell us all about your new love," I said, turning the tables.

The look she gave me was priceless. Much too quickly, she said, "I'm in love with a wonderful, supportive man, and my wild child days are over and done. The end."

Then Bria took a big gulp of wine, finishing off the glass. She couldn't look us in the eye, and I instantly realized she wasn't telling the absolute truth. After all, I had lived with her for almost four years, and I knew when she was lying. And this was one of those moments.

Chapter 13

Brenden

You can do something in an instant that will give you heartache for life.

Seeing Baldwin again was a dream come true. I had thought about her so much the past few years. Sure, I had been married for most of them, but a marriage of convenience didn't and couldn't take the place of true love. Christopher used to tease me about my unconventional male views on love and romance.

I admit I was a traditional type of guy. Ain't no shame in my game. I guess that was why Christopher and I bonded so quickly. We balanced out each other. My mellow, easygoing nature balanced out his maverick tendencies, and in the process we formed a strong bond. One I thought was unbreakable. Sometimes what you thought wasn't necessarily your reality, though.

When I first arrived at Rihanna's home and saw Baldwin standing there in dark denim jeans, a formfitting sweater, and tan snow boots, I thought my heart would literally leap out of my chest because it was pounding so hard. With her short-cropped haircut, flawless brown complexion, she was just as beautiful, if not more so, as I remembered. I had dreamed of staring into her almond-shaped eyes many times. Because of our history together, I realized I wouldn't exactly be

the person she wanted to reunite with, but I didn't realize her greeting would be quite so distant and ice cold.

I manned up and accepted full responsibility that I
had made a lot of mistakes back in the day. We both
did. If I had it to do over, I would make very different
choices. There was something to be said about being
young and dumb. However, the damage was done now,
and there wasn't any going back or turning back the
hands of time. I only hoped that Baldwin would forgive
me so that we could move on.

I didn't know what came over me when I heard her
talking on her cell to her man. I was jealous. I wanted
her to flash that smile and for her eyes to sparkle like
that for me. Like they used to. I guess that was simply
wishful thinking on my part, because Baldwin couldn't
stand the sight of me. After what I did, I couldn't blame
her. Yet she wasn't entirely innocent, either. Each of
us—Bria, Christopher, Rihanna, Baldwin, and I— had
deep histories with each other. That bond would never
be broken, no matter how many years came and went.
I only hoped that the next few days would bring some
form of mending.

*As I slowly eased out of her, making sure the con-
dom was still intact, I tenderly smiled down at her.
"I didn't hurt you, did I?" I asked, propped up on one
elbow as I caressed her face with my other hand.*

*"Not at all," she said, pulling the sheet up to cover
her nakedness. I found her innocence amusing and
refreshing.*

*Naked, I got up and walked into the bathroom to
flush the condom and wash my hands. When I came
back into the bedroom, Baldwin was sitting up, supported by a pillow, watching me intently.*

"What are you smiling about?" she giggled.

"I'm thinking about how beautiful you look lying in my bed with the afterglow of making love," I explained.

She blushed and looked down, unsure of where to rest her eyes.

"You don't realize how beautiful you are, do you?"

She didn't respond. Her timidness aroused me again as I felt my erection growing in length.

"I can't believe I'm no longer a virgin," she said in amazement. "I was going to wait until marriage."

"That's right, madam. You've been defrocked, so I guess that means we have to marry right away," I said jokingly. "Seriously, you aren't sorry about it, are you?"

"Absolutely not. I'm happy you were my first, and it was perfect, just like I imagined it would be. You were gentle and loving and perfect."

We smiled, and I bent to kiss her, parting her lips with my warm tongue. Baldwin pulled the covers back, inviting me into the warmth of her space.

"Talk to me. What are you thinking? Let's make a promise here and now to always be honest with one another," she said.

I lay down and pulled her close. With my arms wrapped snugly around her, I swore our hearts were beating in perfect sync.

"I was thinking how special you are and how I'm lucky to have you in my life," I said.

"Oh, that's so sweet. Same here, baby."

"Are you sure?"

"What kind of question is that? Of course I am, or you wouldn't be lying next to me after devirginizing me," she kidded, gently kissing me on the lips.

"What kind of word is that?"

"One I just made up. I thought it sounded pretty good." She giggled. I loved her laughter and warm spirit.

"I'm happy I met you, Baldwin. The first day I spotted you at the student center, I sensed you were different."

"Same here. You make me smile, and I personally think we were meant to be together," she said, intertwining her fingers with mine and not letting go.

"Even with Christopher's objections? That's my partner and all, but he can't stand the thought of us being together as a couple."

"Even with. He's being protective of me, that's all. Christopher thinks of me as a sister."

"Sister, huh? If you say so."

From that point on, Baldwin and I were inseparable. When you saw Baldwin, you saw me or I wasn't far behind. It was as if the first time we made love, we established ourselves as a couple. Baldwin and I had dated for a couple of months, getting to know one another, which was a first for me, before we slept together. It was well worth the wait. Eventually Christopher came around and approved of our relationship. It wasn't until later, much later, that he committed the ultimate betrayal.

Chapter 14

Brenden

Two people can look at the exact same thing and see something totally different.

After a delicious Southern dinner, courtesy of the girls, everyone pitched in to clean up the kitchen and then retired to the living room. It had been a long day, but I had a lot of nervous energy to release.

Rihanna's mom had called earlier to give us details regarding the home-going service the following day. Mrs. Brown apologized for not coming by to greet us properly, and for not having any food in the refrigerator, but of course, we all understood wholeheartedly. I couldn't imagine how I'd feel if I'd lost my son. Life as I knew it would be over.

The group hadn't been in the living room any longer than ten minutes before a radio was tuned to a local station that played slow jams and oldies from back in the day. Drinks continued to flow, and we were not feeling any pain. Bria and Christopher played the gracious hosts, making sure our glasses remained full.

"Brenden, you have to show us a photo of your son," Bria proclaimed from her seat on the carpeted floor. "I know you have to have one in your wallet."

"As a matter of fact, I do," I said, pulling out my wallet from my back pocket with a big grin plastered across my face, acting like the proud daddy I was.

They took turns passing the photos around as they cooed and aahed. I think my chest was stuck out even farther, if that was humanly possible.

"Damn, man, are you sure you didn't spit him out yourself?" Christopher asked, sitting next to me on the sofa. I watched Baldwin check out the pictures with no expression on her face, then handed them quickly back to Bria.

"Ladies, I know your biological clocks are tick, tick, ticking away, so when are you guys going to have children?" Christopher teased, trying to start something.

"Oh, no, he didn't go there," Bria said, speaking directly to Baldwin. "Christopher, I can't even believe that shit came out of your mouth."

"I know how women get when they are over thirty with no children. My lady is a few years short of thirty, and she constantly reminds me that time is ticking away."

"Women today are having babies much later in life," Bria shared. "I'm not in a rush. Right now my job takes up much of my time."

"Same here. I'm in no rush, and I'm not sure I want any," Baldwin confessed.

"I wouldn't trade my son for anything in the world. I can honestly say my life changed when he was born. My priorities definitely shifted," I said.

Baldwin turned away and looked disinterested. She definitely wasn't making our current situation easy.

The group talked even more, drank some more, spoke of the past—of how we became *the group*. No one spoke of why we parted and went our separate ways after college. Those secrets were kept at bay, lingering on the surface with unspoken words, secrets that were bursting to spring forth their truths.

Everyone spoke fondly of Rihanna, of their genuine love for her. We each had a Rihanna story to share. Most of them brought laughter and good memories. I still couldn't get Baldwin to meet my eyes for more than a few seconds at a time. She spoke in short, clipped sentences, barely addressed me directly, and when she did, she always appeared to be looking slightly over my head. It was like she was afraid of what she'd see or maybe of what I'd see in her eyes.

I longed to be alone with her for just a few minutes. I assumed if we could talk face-to-face, alone, some of her barriers would crumble down. I hoped so. I finally got my chance when she headed upstairs to use the bathroom. I waited a few minutes, not to be too obvious, and then followed. Christopher gave me a nod as I sprinted up the stairs two at a time. My timing was impeccable, because right as I made it to the top of the stairs, she walked out of the bathroom. We were face-to-face and alone. For a moment, I saw the love she once had for me—maybe even the old passion—reflected in her eyes. If so, it was gone in seconds, making me second-guess myself as to whether I had really seen it.

"Oh, sorry," Baldwin said, trying to rush past me in the tight space that we shared. "Excuse me."

"Are you all right?" I asked, noticing her red-rimmed eyes.

She shook her head. "I'm okay. It's just so hard being here in Rihanna's house. I sense her spirit all around us, and everybody is talking and sharing stories about her. Rihanna should be here, not lying cold and lifeless in some funeral home. It's just too much. It's overwhelming," she shared, staring at the floor, biting her bottom lip, which was visibly trembling.

"I realize this is hard on you. It's difficult on all of us, but Rihanna wouldn't want us to be sad. You know that. She'd want us to celebrate her life, not mourn it."

I pulled her into my arms as she attempted to compose herself. I felt her relax for a few moments as she leaned into my chest. I pulled her closer. As if she suddenly realized who she was speaking with and whose arms she was in, I saw and felt her iciness return.

"I'm going to go back downstairs," she said, pulling away abruptly. "Excuse me," she said, wiping tears from her eyes with the back of her hand, trying to step around me without touching me.

"Baldwin?"

She didn't respond, just kept walking.

"Baldwin, please."

She turned around with a cold scowl. "What do you want, Brenden?"

"Listen, I can't do this," I said, throwing up my hands in surrender.

"Do what, Brenden? I'm not sure I understand what you are talking about," she said, her diction clipped.

"Baldwin, come on. I remember you were always stubborn, but give me a break. Damn, I'm trying to make an effort."

"Well, don't bother. How about that? I didn't ask you to make an effort. What is the saying? Too little, too late." Baldwin continued to stare me down, making me feel like I was the filthy gum on the bottom of her shoe.

"Come on, Baldwin. Hear me out. You owe me that much."

She then laughed. A strong, venomous laugh.

"You think so? The nerve of you. Unbelievable."

"I'm just saying—"

"I don't owe you a damn thing. You crossed that line and forfeited that right many years ago. So don't tell me what I owe you," she said forcefully.

"And you did the same. I tried to contact you several times."

"For what, Brenden? The damage was already done. Like I said before, too little, too late."

"What do you want from me, Baldwin? Tell me so I can make it better. I want to make it right, once and for all."

"Absolutely nothing, Brenden. Not a damn thing. I want nothing from you. Does that answer your question? Am I clear?"

We stared each other down. I saw so much pain in her eyes; I was not sure what she saw in mine. Anger, love, lust, longing, hurt perhaps.

"Honestly, I didn't mean to hurt you back then. It was just after you did—"

"I don't want to hear it," she screeched, placing her hands over her ears. "Stop it!"

I paused. Confused. Upset. Finally I said, "Can we at least be cordial to each other through the next couple of days? That's all I ask."

"That I can do. With pleasure. I'll make a deal with you. You stay away from me, and I'll do the same."

With that, she turned and literally stomped down the stairs like a raging inferno. I was left standing there, trying to make some sense out of what had just occurred.

Chapter 15

Christopher

We are responsible for what we do, no matter how we feel.

I was not quite sure what happened upstairs between Brenden and Baldwin. They acted like two immature college students—even though those years were long gone. Baldwin needed to give the man a break, and Brenden needed to man up and admit his hand in what went down back in the day. That was just my ten cents. I admit, in the beginning I didn't think they were right for each other; they had too many differences, too many obstacles in their path that spelled disaster.

After witnessing firsthand the genuine love they showed whenever they were together, which was all the time, they won me over. It wasn't like they were going to listen to me, anyway, but I thought they appreciated my approval.

The mood in the house shifted after their confrontation, went downhill. Everyone took to their separate corners, with Baldwin and Brenden as far away from each other as possible, and reflected. There was nothing like the death of a family member or friend to make you think about your own mortality. When it was that close to you, you couldn't deny it.

Still drinking, we did our individual things. Bria was in the kitchen, whispering to someone on her cell. She was speaking so softly, with a few outbursts here and there, that it sparked my interest as to whom she was talking to.

Brenden, seated back on the sofa, had taken out his BlackBerry and was going through e-mails and texts, while Baldwin, on the love seat, pretended to peruse a magazine, when in fact she was checking him out. I saw baby girl giving him the eye on the sly as I sat across from her in the wing chair.

I texted a few people regarding work matters and then got caught up in some reflecting of my own. Unbeknownst to the others, I had seen Rihanna a few times over the years. My travels all over the country brought me to the Raleigh-Durham area quite often. In fact, it was one of my regular stops. My agency was constantly scouting the universities here because they produced some of the best players in the nation and this area was known for going all out to support collegiate sports. Occasionally, I'd stop by Rihanna's, and she'd cook a mouthwatering meal, we'd have good conversations about the old times, catch up with each other's lives, and eventually one thing would lead to another.

As I went in and out of her in slow, fluid motions, she stared at me with an innocent, awed expression. Like she couldn't believe I was there with her, in her bed. Inside her. I knew she had a big crush on me during college, but I wasn't attracted to her that way. Rihanna was my friend. My buddy. My ace boon coon.

"Does that feel good? Am I hitting it the way you like?" I asked, already knowing the answer.

I saw her eyes half closed as she struggled to keep her moans at bay. I knew I was whipping it on her royally and she was too timid to totally enjoy it and let loose.

"Talk to me, Rihanna," I said, spreading her legs wider with my knees.

She still didn't respond. I was used to dominating my women in the bedroom, having them moaning and squirming, trying to get away from what I threw on them. I was that good, and I had a long list of women who could cosign to that fact.

I kissed and nibbled her neck and eased my way down to suckle and touch one of the prettiest breasts I had ever seen. I stroked a nipple with my thumb as I teased the other with my tongue.

"Ahhh."

I looked into her face and saw pure ecstasy.

"Yeah, that's it. That's your weakness."

I slowly stroked her deeper as I sucked and tweaked her nipples.

"Ahhh, Christopher. I've waited so long for this."

Rihanna and I came at almost the same time, and judging by the jubilant expression on her face, she was definitely happy. From that point on, it was on. We became friends with benefits. I hadn't been with too many big girls before, but from what I could see, she could work it as well, if not better, than any of these skinny chicks. The last time we were together intimately, I knew our arrangement was coming to an end.

"Why are you so quiet?" I asked, caressing her brownish red hair, which she wore in stylish single-strand braids.

"I was just thinking."

"About what?"

"It's silly."

"You know you can talk to me about anything."

"I was just thinking about you and me."

"You and I? Really?"

My body tensed, because I had heard different versions of this speech throughout the years. The woman, usually after I had sexed her, was ready to commit to a relationship and I wasn't. The end result was always the same.

"What about us?" I asked cautiously. "I think we have a good thing going, don't you?"

Rihanna smiled that hundred-watt smile that spotlighted those deep dimples that I adored. "What am I to you?"

"What do you mean?"

"Come on, Christopher. You know what I'm asking."

"We kick it when I'm in town, and we have a good time together. We have history."

"We never go anywhere."

"Because you always volunteer to cook. Besides your cooking beats any four-star restaurant I've ever been to. And when I'm here, I like to chill."

"You have never asked if I'd like to go out. Not even once," she said and pouted, giving me her full attention.

I decided to flip the conversation and put her on the defensive. "Don't you like how we make each other feel?"

"Christopher, I love the sex. You're a wonderful lover. But . . ."

"But what?" I asked, gently touching her face.

"I feel like a booty call or jump-off."

"You shouldn't. I've never given you any reason to feel that way. I don't come over to your house late at night, expecting sex. I don't step to you like that. You mean much more to me than that, Rihanna."

"No, you come over, eat my food, watch a movie, have sex, and then leave. You rarely stay over and spend the night."

I looked up at the ceiling. "I guess I assumed we had an understanding."

"What understanding? That you could fuck me behind closed doors whenever you were in town, without a commitment, Christopher?"

I didn't comment, didn't know what to say.

"I may be a big girl, and I know I'm not your type, but I'm not desperate, Christopher," she said, turning her back to me.

"Rihanna, you know it's not even like that. I'm not ashamed to be seen with you in public, if that's what you're saying. Why would you think such a thing?"

I saw sadness reflected in her eyes as she turned to face me again.

"It's always the same. It's been this way my entire life. I have a pretty face, so men think I'm good enough to fuck behind closed doors, but it always ends there. I never seem to have a happy ending."

I pulled her close. She jerked away, like she couldn't stand my touch anymore.

"Don't."

"Why not? I can't touch you now?"

She ignored my questions. "Do you know I've had a crush on you since the very first time I saw you on campus, entering the humanities building?"

I remained silent.

"I admired you from afar. Played it safe by being your friend. I knew I'd never have a man like you—a pretty boy. So I took what I could. Your friendship."

I started to speak, but she hushed me.

"And now, here we are. Did you know when we first started sleeping together that I went on a diet for you, *trying to change myself? I don't do that. I decided years ago to love myself just the way I am. Take me or leave me was my motto."*

"And you are pretty just the way you are."

"But I'm still simply a booty call to you, because I don't fit your rail-thin glamour girl type."

"I've told you it's not even like that, Rihanna. I'm having the time of my life. I have a great job, I'm making good money, and I'm not ready to settle down with any woman yet."

"I know, Christopher. Maybe one day, right?" she said with the saddest smile. "You don't have to explain."

Rihanna and I slept together one more time that night. For once, I spent the night. We fell asleep holding each other, and the next morning she fixed me a hearty breakfast, then served it to me in bed before I left to catch my plane.

Her last words were "I hope you never experience the pain of loving someone so badly and they don't love you back. But then again . . . I guess you have." With her words haunting me, I left to drive to the airport.

There was one. Back in the day.

After that, I called her a few times when I was in town, just to check up on her and to see if I could come by, but she always said she was busy. She ended each call with "I love you, Christopher. Probably always will."

Chapter 16

Bria

It's taking me a long time to become the person I want to be.

I whispered into my cell phone. "It's strange being here, actually staying in the home of my deceased friend. . . . No one has changed. Not much. I couldn't believe it, but basically we eased right back into our old roles, like we had seen each other just last night."

"That's good," Terry responded. "I knew you were anxious about seeing them again."

As I leaned against the granite kitchen counter, I peered into the living room. Baldwin, Brenden, and Christopher were caught up in their own worlds. Not paying me a bit of attention. *Good.*

"Have you told them yet?"

I immediately stiffened.

"Hello? Are you still there?"

"I'm here," I said.

"Have you?"

"No, baby. Not yet. The group settled in, had dinner and probably too many drinks, and it never felt like an appropriate time."

"When then?"

"I'm not sure. Everyone is pretty tired tonight. It's been a long day, and I'm sure we'll be going to bed soon. The home-going is tomorrow afternoon."

"Always making excuses, huh?"

"I'm not, baby. Just trust me and be patient a little longer," I whispered.

"Are you ashamed of our life together?"

"Absolutely not. How could you ask me that? I've given up my family for you. If that doesn't prove my love, then I don't know what will."

"Well, tell them. You told me that these were the three people that you have felt the closest to during your lifetime."

"They were. Still, it's not that easy, baby."

"I don't see the problem. Tell them and get it over with."

"I will. I promise. I'll talk to you tomorrow, okay? I'm tired."

"I love you so much, Bria, and I don't mean to be hard on you, but I want us to share our love with the world. You are my everything, and I want everyone to know it. I want to scream it from the rooftop."

Before I hung up, I said, "I love you too, baby. I can't wait to get back home to you. I miss you."

I composed myself, closing my eyes for a few seconds and regrouping. It was funny how when old friends were reunited, you tended to revert back to the title or label you once held. I was always the wild child of the group. I had completely forgotten that nickname until Christopher ever so happily reminded me of it.

I'd be the first to admit I did a lot of things in college that I was not proud of. We all had our regrets, and my sleeping around was one of them. It was like I was trying to validate myself by screwing as many men as possible, and on a college campus that wasn't too hard to achieve. At least that was what my therapist told me . . . my college years were spent running from my true identity.

I was forever grateful I didn't catch an STD or, worse, AIDS. Ain't no coming back from that shit. I was one of the lucky ones, living in God's favor. My mother, who I hadn't spoken to in over two and a half years, would say otherwise. She just knew my soul was going straight to hell in a handbasket, because she had a pipeline straight to God. Now I just needed to come up with the nerve to tell the group that I was a lesbian. I knew I didn't have to, but I wanted to. It was important to me to come out to them.

I think a part of me always knew, even as a child. I had fought it for so long, and I was so tired. I simply couldn't continue to live a lie. Now I had a beautiful partner, Terry. She was the love of my life, and I'd literally give up my life for hers. Our only problem was my resistance to openly living the gay lifestyle. Terry had been out most of her young adult life, but this was new for me, and it was hard for her to understand my reluctance to come out completely.

I thought back to one of the last conversations I had with Rihanna. At the time, I was seriously debating if I wanted Terry to move in. That would change everything and announce to the world who and what I was. I was absolutely terrified, and I really didn't have anyone I could talk to—not about that, anyway.

One Friday night Terry had literally given me an ultimatum and had left my townhome in tears, and I had fretted most of the weekend over the thought of losing her. Before I could stop myself, I picked up the phone and dialed directory assistance, and within a few minutes Rihanna was on the other line.

"May I speak with Rihanna?"

"This is she."

"It's me, Bria. I hope I'm not calling too late."

"No, not at all. I'm just surprised to hear from you. Believe it or not, you've been on my mind lately."

"I apologize, but I never was the type to pick up a phone and call my friends. And with work and . . ." I made a weak attempt at excuses.

"Better late than never. No need to explain. How are you? How have you been?"

With those simple words coming from someone who genuinely cared, I broke down again. I surprised myself at the depth of my anguish.

"Bria, what's wrong?"

I was sobbing loudly by then, trying to find my voice and feeling embarrassed all at the same time.

"You know you can talk to me. Whatever it is, it isn't the end of the world, sweetie."

"It feels like it is," I said between sobs.

"Well, let's talk about it. We can sort it out, you and me."

With that, I told her everything, and you know what? She didn't judge me. She didn't think less of me; she didn't think I was some sort of freak; she didn't think I would burn in eternal hellfires. What she did was ask a few questions, which put my situation in perspective.

"Do you love her?"

"Yes. With all my heart."

"Does she love you?"

"Yes. She tells me she does, and her actions prove it."

"Do you make each other happy?"

"Without a doubt."

"Do you think of her first thing each morning, when you awaken, and is she the last thing on your mind before you go to sleep?"

I laughed. "Actually, yes, to both questions."

"Can you imagine life without her?"

"I absolutely cannot."

"Well, there's your answer, sweetie. You had it all along."

I didn't say anything. I was reflecting on what Rihanna had pointed out to me.

"Bria, live your life, and stop letting others live it for you. Life is too short. Too short to worry about small-minded, ignorant people and what they have to say or think. This is your life, not theirs, and you only get one."

I remained silent, listened to her calming spirit and affirming words. Letting them sink in.

"Bria? Are you there? Do you hear me?"

"I'm taking in every word."

"Do you realize how rare it is to find love, real love, during your lifetime? Embrace it, girl, and don't let go. Hold on with all your might."

We hung up shortly after that, and I followed Rihanna's advice and never looked back. Terry moved in a month later. I gained the love of my life but unfortunately lost my mother in the process. She couldn't and wouldn't accept my lifestyle. That was a hard cross to bear.

I wish I could say Terry and I had had a fairy-tale life, but then I'd be lying. We definitely had had our ups and downs. I still had some issues with my sexuality, but whenever I was feeling low, I always thought back to those questions Rihanna asked and realized my answers hadn't changed.

Chapter 17

Baldwin

Sometimes the people you expect to kick you when you're down will be the ones to help you get back up.

I discreetly checked out Brenden from the corner of my eye as I pretended to read an article in the *Better Homes and Gardens* magazine that I had picked up from the coffee table. Every so often, I'd look up and take another peek at him as he scanned through e-mails on his BlackBerry.

He was still a handsome man, not drop-dead gorgeous, but very attractive. Easy on the eyes. I was still peeved over our argument upstairs. I didn't mean to blow up like that and surprised myself, but he stood there acting like he was the only rational one back then. Not.

And I couldn't believe Brenden was a dad. Earlier, when I'd looked at those photos from his wallet, something tugged inside my heart. His son was absolutely adorable, and I was sure Brenden was the perfect dad. When he spoke of his son, love radiated outward. He couldn't contain it. Just like Christopher said, it looked like he'd spit his son, Jordan, out. There was definitely no denying him.

I didn't know if we got caught up in the reason we had reunited, but it was obvious the mood in the room had changed. Music from the local radio station still played softly in the background, and wine was still being consumed, but everybody had suddenly and unexpectedly retreated into their own private shells. It was obvious we enjoyed our close proximity, because no one ventured upstairs, but inner reflection was at play now. Being in the group's presence comforted me.

I thought back to a few years earlier, to the only contact I had had with Rihanna since we said our final good-byes and promised to keep in touch after graduation day. Out of the blue, a letter came in the mail. At the time, I found it strange because, seriously, who actually took the time to sit down and pen an actual letter on fancy stationery these days? That was like a lost art. So it immediately caught my attention when I retrieved it from the mailbox. There wasn't a return address on the outside of the envelope, and my info had been typed on the front.

As soon as I tore open the envelope and saw the familiar script writing, I instantly knew whom it was from. Rihanna. I immediately recognized Rihanna's handwriting. I remembered how it used to look big, bold, and curvy, like it was jumping off the page. Years might come and go, but certain things stayed with you. The letter read:

Dear Baldwin,

I don't know if this letter will reach you, but I sincerely hope it does. I know this must be a shock, hearing from me after all these years. Even though we haven't spoken in a while, I miss you and still reminisce on the fun times we once shared.

I don't know if you realized it or not, but I looked up to you back then. I admired you so much. I hope you don't find this letter to be inap-

propriate, but I wanted to touch base because I wanted to share something with you.

In case you are wondering, I got your address from the college alumni directory. I don't know how to begin, so I'll jump right in. I ran into Brenden a couple of days ago—he looked good, same ole Brenden. He said he was passing through town, had some downtime during a layover, and ventured out to a local restaurant for lunch. Seeing him again brought back many memories. Good ones.

We chatted. Brenden asked about you. Told me he had tried to contact you years ago, but you never responded to his calls, and eventually you changed your number. Listen, I know it's none of my business, but I just hated to see him like that. He's not in a good place. His marriage is on the rocks, and he said he was seriously considering a divorce. His eyes lit up only when he spoke of you.

I'm not trying to get in the middle of anything or place you in an uncomfortable situation. I don't even know what path life has led you down. I just wish the two of you could find closure. God placed it on my heart to write this, and you can do with it as you see fit. Just know that I care about both of you. You are still in my heart, in a good place. I remember how hurt you were one of the last times we talked, years ago, but Baldwin, you can't carry unforgiveness in your spirit forever. People make mistakes. This was written with love.

Friends always, Rihanna

I never did respond to Rihanna's letter. I read it and tossed it in the nearest trash can. Thinking about it now, I felt bad, but at the time, I thought she needed to mind her own business and stay out of mine. She was always handing out unsolicited advice. Now, I knew she meant well. As for Brenden, I didn't have an ounce of compassion for his situation. He made his choice, and now he had to live with it, the same way as I lived with mine. I didn't have any sympathy then, and I didn't have any now.

Chapter 18

Baldwin

I believe you can keep going long after you can't.

The morning of the funeral was glum and dreary, which matched my mood exactly. I had tossed and turned most of the night, not getting much sleep. Events from my past rewound over and again, as if I was watching one of those old black-and-white movie clips. Finally at seven, I gave up, rolled over on my back, sighed, and stared at the ceiling for a while. The house was still. Quiet. Peaceful. I sighed again. Bria had her back turned to me, and I thought she was soundly sleeping, so I didn't want to disturb her.

"You can't sleep either, huh?" Bria asked, slowly turning toward me.

"No. Too many memories. I've been wide awake for over an hour now."

"Today's the day," she said.

"Yep."

"Rihanna's mom said relatives and friends will start arriving around eleven to line up for the procession."

"Okay." I sighed loudly.

"Mrs. Brown wants us to ride in one of the limos," she said quietly.

Bria's head was on her pillow, and mine on my pillow. I noticed her head scarf had come off during the course of the night. Our heads turned inward, and we faced each other. There was a moment of silence.

"I guess we'd better get up and moving," I said, throwing back the covers but not moving. This was surreal. Rihanna's funeral was in a few hours.

"Yep." Bria hopped up, headed to the bathroom, and closed the door. When I heard the shower turn on, I finally got up and lazily stretched.

Walking downstairs in my pink pj's and fuzzy slippers, I found Brenden sitting at the kitchen table. If he hadn't looked up and smiled, I was sure I would have turned around and quietly headed back upstairs until he left, or at least until someone else came downstairs to join us.

"Good morning," he said, holding up a bag and a cup of Starbucks coffee.

That brought a genuine smile to my face. "Thank you," I said, reaching for the coffee like it was my lifeline.

"You're very welcome. I remembered you pretty much couldn't start your day without a cup of mocha. You were never a morning person."

I laughed despite myself. "Still true."

"Some things never change," he said. "There are bagels, cream cheese, and muffins in the bag as well. Help yourself."

I reached into the paper bag and pulled out a raisin bagel. I quietly sat down across from him. Brenden returned to read the local paper and didn't bother with early morning conversation. That was a good thing, because I knew I wasn't up for it. Not this morning. We sat in a peaceful silence with heavy hearts.

Eventually Bria and Christopher made their way downstairs, said their good mornings, and grabbed coffee, juice, and a muffin and bagel. They joined us at the table, looking frazzled from the night before.

"What's the plan for today?" Christopher asked, looking at each of us after he sat down and started spreading cream cheese on his bagel.

"We need to be dressed and ready by eleven," Bria informed us as she bit into her blueberry muffin.

The group sat in silence for a few minutes, the realization of what would happen in a few hours sinking in.

"They ran Rihanna's obituary in the paper this morning," Brenden said, passing the newspaper around. "Her entire life was summed up in a few lines."

The house phone, which sat on an end table, started ringing, pulling us out of our reverie. Bria ran to answer it.

"Hello. . . . Good morning, Mrs. Brown. . . . Yes. We are up and eating a light breakfast. . . . Uh-huh. Sure. That will work. We'll see you soon then. . . . Uh-huh. . . . Again, thank you for your hospitality. We appreciate it and can't imagine what you are going through, and yet you are still looking out for us. We'll see you soon."

Bria hung up and slowly turned to look at us. "I guess we should start getting dressed. That was Mrs. Brown on the phone, and she wanted to know if any of us wanted to say a few words at the funeral. I told her I'd ask you guys and let her know when she gets here."

We nodded in unison and slowly rose from the table, one at a time, to get ready for the home-going. I was simply going through the motions.

Approximately two hours later, we were dressed solemnly in black, waiting like small children in the living room. Bria and I had on black dresses with black pumps, and Christopher and Brenden wore black suits with crisp white shirts and dark ties. We clustered together in our space, not really saying much. Yet the silence and sharing the same space were comforting.

As expected, family and friends started arriving at the modest house. There were so many people that some had to stand outside because there were not enough space inside. Mrs. Brown walked in and greeted us with a warm smile, hugs, and welcoming arms. She was definitely a mature version of Rihanna; the resemblance was uncanny. She was stout and solid, with her salt-and-pepper hair pulled back in a tight bun. She was exactly as I remembered her.

"I'm so glad y'all could make it," she said with a slight Southern drawl, strolling to the sofa and taking a seat.

"We couldn't have not shown up to show our respects," I said for all of us.

"Rihanna, after all these years, still talked about y'all," she continued.

No one responded.

"Rihanna was planning a reunion before she got sick. Then, during her illness, she simply didn't have the strength to pull it together, but she never forgot you."

"And we never forgot her," Bria assured her. "That's why we're here."

"It's so good to see y'all. You've grown into such wonderful adults, but I always knew you would," Mrs. Brown said as another wave of hugs broke loose. "Brenden and Christopher, if you don't mind, I need y'all to follow me and help us get those folding chairs in the house so that everyone can have somewhere to sit," she added, holding on to my arm to pull herself up from the sofa cushion.

"Yes, ma'am," they said at the same time, following behind her, willing to help out in any way possible.

"Such strong, handsome men. I'm so proud of you," she said, patting each in turn on the back.

Before we knew it, it was time to line up and prepare to leave for the church. An elderly, gray-haired man with a weatherworn face led everyone in prayer before we left for our cars.

"Link hands with the person standing next to you and form a circle," he said in a gravelly voice. That placed me in between Bria and Brenden. Bria sought out my left hand, and I reluctantly reached for Brenden's with my right hand.

"All heads bowed, eyes closed and hearts clear."

"Heavenly Father, today we are saying our final good-byes, for now, to a young woman who brought much love and happiness to so many lives during her short stay here on earth. Lord, we can't begin to question the whys or hows or question why you saw fit to take this precious angel from us so soon. It was your will. It wasn't meant for us to understand. We are just thankful that she touched our lives in a positive manner, and we are all better people from knowing her.

"Dear God, bless her mother, keep her wrapped up in your loving, strong arms, and help her to understand that this isn't good-bye. She will see her baby, Rihanna, one day. She's in a better place now but lives on in our hearts. She's at peace and no longer in pain. Bless these relatives and friends who have come from near and far. Give them comfort in knowing that we aren't here to cry and grieve. No, dear Father, Rihanna wouldn't want that. No, she wouldn't. We are here to celebrate and rejoice in the short life she lived. Let's send mighty praises up to heaven that proclaim how blessed we were to know her. Amen."

"Amen," everyone chanted in unison.

I noticed Brenden was hesitant in releasing my hand. I looked over at him and saw a flicker of tears glistening in his eyes.

"Everything's going to be okay," I said quietly, rubbing his back. "We're here. The group is here."

I noticed Bria had her arms wrapped tightly around Christopher's waist as small white flowers were pinned on our lapels and we were led to the awaiting black limo.

Someone started singing "His Eye Is on the Sparrow," and suddenly I wasn't so sure if I was going to make it through this. Such a harsh wave of sadness and loss hit me, like a punch in the pit of my stomach. Out of nowhere, I felt Brenden gently reach for my hand and intertwine our fingers, and I didn't pull away. I simply relaxed as a sense of peace and protection overtook me.

Chapter 19

Baldwin

Credentials on the wall do not make you a decent human being.

The funeral lived up to its name. It was most definitely a home-going service for our girl, Rihanna Brown. Certainly there were tears, but through it all there was a sense of happiness and rejoicing—and wonderment over a beautiful spirit that had graced and touched each of our lives.

The group was seated on the third pew from the front of the church, Bria and I in the middle. Brenden was to my right, and Christopher to her left. They were our cloaks of protection during the entire service. My tears flowed freely, and throughout it all, Brenden never let go of my hand. In fact, at one point, he wrapped his arm protectively around my shoulder as my head rested on his. I never could have made it without him, without the group by my side.

Beautiful, colorful, fragrant flowers and plants were positioned everywhere the eyes could behold. They shrouded the small church with encompassing arms. It was standing room only, and people had come from high and low to say their farewells. There was such a deep sense of love that enveloped everyone that it was almost tangible.

Right before the eulogy was to be delivered, the congregation was asked if there was anyone who would like to say a few words. The group was choked up, but to my surprise and amazement, I saw Brenden slowly rise and walk determinedly to the front of the church. He glanced over at me, hesitant for a moment, and I nodded and smiled faintly. He cleared his throat and proceeded to speak straight from his heart.

"To Mrs. Brown and family members, to the pastor, members, visitors, and friends, I couldn't have missed today if my life depended upon it. I had to say my final good-bye. I met Rihanna during my freshman year of college, at State University, and it was an instant bonding of friendship and respect. We simply clicked. And I can tell you now, I am almost thirty-two years old and I can count on one hand the number of people I have simply clicked with. I believe people are placed in our lives for a reason and sometimes for just a season.

"I loved Rihanna. How could you not? My one regret is that I never told her. I think she knew it. I hope so. She was the sweetest person I have ever met. Rihanna was always placing others before her own needs, and I don't believe there was a selfish bone in her body. At the time I was young and probably took her for granted. In fact, I know I did. Now that I'm older and hopefully wiser, I realize what a rare treasure, a true blessing I had. A famous French author once said, 'However rare true love may be, it is less so than true friendship.'

"Rihanna taught me a great deal, so many life lessons, but most of all she taught me humility. She used to say all the time how you cannot judge a person until you've walked in their shoes for a day. I couldn't relate to that statement back then, but now I can. I can honestly say I became a better person from knowing her. I'll miss you, Rihanna, every day, and I finally get what you were trying to tell me. Lesson learned. You are gone but never forgotten."

As loud hand clapping and amens erupted throughout the sanctuary, Brenden walked over and kissed Mrs. Brown on the cheek and returned to his seat. His emotional and heartfelt speech had touched everyone, including me. More tears fell.

"Saints, say amen to that young man's moving words. What a wonderful, beautiful testament and tribute to Sister Rihanna Brown." The middle-aged preacher beamed. "Yes, indeed. Amen, amen, amen. Yes, Lord," he shouted, jumping up and down on the heels of his feet, visibly shaken. "Is there anyone else who'd like to speak?" he asked, looking around and pausing for a few seconds as he perused the audience.

As if I was having an out-of-body experience, I found myself walking slowly, but steadily, to the front of the small southern Baptist church. As I stared out at the sea of faces, such incredible emotion overtook my spirit that I had to pause for a moment to collect my thoughts. I took a deep breath to steady myself and spoke from within as countless nameless faces peered back in anticipation.

"It's said you never miss what you have until it's gone. Very true. I can attest to everything Brenden stated because we were all best of friends at State University. Rihanna and I met during our freshman year and also had an undeniable connection from the very beginning. It was like we had always known one another. There was a sense of belonging when we were together, a sense of connectedness. Family.

"The one thing that will always stand out about her was that humongous smile. Rihanna had a gorgeous one, and she'd look at you and you couldn't help but smile back. Rihanna could always find the good in even the most negative situations. Sometimes I envied that. She was our Little Miss Sunshine. She'd wake up in a good mood, humming, singing, and just happy to be alive another day. She was like that. Rihanna was like a sister to me, the sister I never had. Rest in peace, our Little Miss Sunshine. I'll love you always and forever."

Chapter 20

Bria

Brenden's and Baldwin's words brought another round of waterworks, swiftly streaming down my face in cascades. I didn't bother to wipe the tears away anymore. Sitting in the church, with Rihanna's open casket less than fifty feet from where I sat, was unbearable. I kept thinking that any minute someone was going to jump out with TV cameras and declare that this was all a big practical joke. Ha, ha, ha. Rihanna loved playing jokes back in the day; she used to pull off some good ones too.

Stepping out of the shower to find your clothes missing wasn't funny at the time, but it was hilarious now. Yeah, sprinting to my dorm room buck naked, only to find it locked, just as two guys walked up . . . absolutely freaking priceless.

I kept hoping Rihanna was going to walk in and claim her spot, by Baldwin and me, with Christopher and Brenden on the ends. Our bookends. They had always been protective of the girls in the group. True gentlemen. Those days seemed long ago, another lifetime.

Other words were spoken in tribute, and beautiful hymns were sung by the choir, whose members were adorned in royal blue robes with gold trim. Soon the preacher stepped to the pulpit to deliver the eulogy, and it was at that point that my mind drifted back to a conversation from years gone by.

"How can you tell if a guy likes you or not?" Rihanna asked shyly. She was always shy when it came to the opposite sex.

She and I were lounging around in her dorm room on a lazy Sunday afternoon. I think Baldwin was somewhere off with Brenden. And who knew where Christopher was.

"What kind of question is that? You are a grown-ass woman, and you don't know how to tell if the opposite sex is interested?" I asked, kidding her.

"I haven't had as much dating experience as you," she said without judgment.

I looked up from my spot on the twin bed. She was casually flipping through a magazine on the bed adjacent to mine, but I knew she was dead serious.

"Well, does he want to be around you all the time?"

"Sort of. Well, yeah. Usually we are around other people, hanging out."

"Does he talk to you, pay attention to what you have to say?"

"I think so."

"Does he smile when he sees you? Does his face light up?" I asked.

"Yes."

"It sounds like he likes you, girl."

"I'm not so sure about that. I think he considers me only a friend, which is the story of my life. If another person tells me that I have a pretty face, I don't know what I'll do." She sighed heavily.

I didn't comment on Rihanna's last words. I didn't know what to say. I knew she had struggled with her weight and was always on the diet of the week. "Who is this guy?" I asked instead. I had a pretty good idea already.

Rihanna hesitated. "It doesn't matter, Bria. I'll never have a chance with him. He doesn't like girls my size."

"How do you know?" I asked.

"Because I've seen the pencil-thin girls he's dated. He likes them slim and anorexic."

I laughed. "You never know, girl. You never know."

She sighed again and continued to turn the pages of the magazine. "No, believe me, I do."

"Rihanna has a secret crush," I chanted, jumping up off the bed, dancing around the small dorm room. "Rihanna has a crush."

"You are so crazy, Bria. Stop. You're embarrassing me."

"I bet he makes you wet every time you see him."

She blushed and looked at the floor.

"You can tell me, girl."

"He does," she whispered as our eyes met when she looked back up.

"Do you think he has a big dick?"

"Bria!"

"What? I'm just asking. The bigger the better. I know you have snuck a glance at his crotch imprint. You don't want to be all in love with this man and find out later that he's working with a dick the size of your pinkie finger."

Rihanna doubled over, laughing at my silliness, and just like that the subject was changed.

Over the next couple of hours, Rihanna and I giggled, carried on like typical schoolgirls, and caught up on campus gossip. I was secretly delighted that Rihanna was infatuated with someone, because she deserved to find happiness and come out of her dating shell.

I had a talk with Christopher a few weeks later, when we were chilling at his spot. I was sprawled across his bed at the apartment he shared with Brenden about a half mile off campus. I was turned in his direction, and he was lying on his back, staring ahead, with textbooks discarded at his feet.

"You do know that Rihanna has a huge crush on you, dude?" I questioned.

"Does she?" he asked nonchalantly.

"Come on, Christopher. This is real talk. You know she does. You see the way she looks at you with those big brown puppy dog eyes, and she hangs on your every damn word. You have to know unless you're totally blind."

"What exactly do you want me to do about it, Bria?" he asked, looking at me now.

"I'm not asking you to do anything. I'm simply informing you, as if you didn't already know. How do you feel about that?"

"What do you mean? Rihanna's cool. I love her like a little sister, but you know she's not my type. Besides, I'd never fuck her and mess up the friendship we share. You know how you women get once you've gotten the dick."

"That may very well be the case, but she is feeling you. So now you know."

"And there is absolutely nothing I can do about that. She'll get over me eventually."

"Oh, I forgot, you love 'em and leave 'em. Right? You have a trail of broken hearts you've left behind on campus. 'Wham, bam, thank you, ma'am' is the motto you live by."

"What's wrong with that? I'm young, single, good-looking, and a man. Rihanna will find someone, but you are one to talk, Bria. How much dick have you gone through on this campus?"

"I admit you and I are two peas in a pod. Sex is just sex to us, but Rihanna doesn't operate like that. She believes in romance and the knight in shining armor riding in to whisk her away. Sex is special to her. If she likes you, it is because you are special in her eyes, Christopher."

"I don't know what to tell you, Wild Child. She's not my type and much too good of a friend to become involved with the likes of me."

I closed my eyes and turned onto my stomach, enjoying a lazy Sunday afternoon. "I'm too sleepy to study."

"Well, tell me about your friend Tiffany. I'd love to hook up with her."

"I bet you would." I laughed into the pillow.

"Put in a good word for me, as if I need it, though." He laughed and stroked his goatee. "I've seen her checking me out on the sly."

"You are one conceited motherfucker, but we'll see," I said and secretly smiled.

Chapter 21

Christopher

Our background and circumstances may have influenced who we are, but we are responsible for who we become.

Throughout most of the service, I was in another zone. My physical body was there, but my mind was elsewhere. I honestly couldn't tell you much of anything that was shared by the pastor, and I only vaguely recall details of Brenden's and Baldwin's comments about Rihanna's life and our friendship. Mostly I simply hung on to Bria for dear life. She probably thought I was consoling her, which I was, but she didn't realize she was my lifeline.

I had so much guilt over the fact that I never had the opportunity to explain to Rihanna that I was afraid of the kind of love she offered. I realized she thought I was using her as a booty call when I passed through North Carolina, but really I wasn't. Her love scared me. Her complete admiration, dedication, and loyalty, I wasn't used to that. I wasn't used to receiving it or giving it back. So I pulled away and hurt her in the process. If I had known of her illness, I would have been there for her. If only I had known. Hindsight is twenty-twenty.

That wasn't the only time I had hurt Rihanna. Our senior year was the first time. After having a conversation with Bria about Rihanna's crush, to be honest, I didn't think anything else about it, and life went on as before. My sole focus became getting into Bria's friend Tiffany's panties, because I found her a challenge. She had transferred from a smaller college and hadn't fallen for my charm, wit, and good looks yet. All that changed soon enough. Bria helped me out with that dilemma on the night of my birthday.

It was a chilly late Friday night, and I had literally started partying Monday. I figured I'd celebrate my twenty-first birthday with a bang, literally. For an entire week I had been with a different girl each day. Hell, you only lived once. Friday I had partied most of the night away at my frat's old-school party and had returned home to a dark, empty apartment. Brenden was spending the night with Baldwin, so I had the place all to myself, and sex was on my mind when there was a loud knock at the front door.

I stumbled to the door, more than a bit buzzed, and swung it wide open, ready to get on Brenden's back about not having his damn key. He was always forgetting or misplacing it. Besides, he was supposed to be holed up in some hotel by now, fucking Baldwin.

"Hey, Christopher. Happy birthday," Bria said with a huge mischievous smile. "I brought Tiffany by to officially meet you. You had too much going on at the party."

Suddenly the girl of my latest fantasy, my flavor of the week, stepped forward from behind Bria. I blinked a couple of times, thinking I was seeing things in my intoxicated state, but she was still there. Front and center. Big ass, big breasts, and a big smile plastered on her juicy lips, which she licked seductively.

"Hey, Christopher," she gushed, kissing me on the cheek. "I hear it's your birthday. Happy birthday."

I nodded, motioning for them to come in. "Thanks. It is. Did you bring me a present?"

"Now that you ask, actually I did," Tiffany said, walking boldly up to me and planting a kiss on my lips as she stroked between my legs.

Her boldness caught me off guard, but not for long.

"Hmmm, I think I can definitely work with that big package you're carrying. You down?" she asked. "I'm your present. Wanna unwrap me?"

I looked from her to Bria, assuming this was a cruel joke. Bria innocently smiled and nodded.

"Hell, yeah!" I said, eagerly pulling off my shirt, reaching for her hand, and leading her toward the bedroom.

"Wait, wait! Hold up! There is a small catch," she said, stopping in mid-step and looking mischievously in Bria's direction.

"What's the catch?" I asked.

"You get two for one tonight."

"What do you mean?"

"Exactly what I said. Tonight's your lucky night, birthday boy. You get to fuck both of us."

I glanced at Bria and for the first time noticed she was high, eyes glazed over. I grabbed her arm and pulled her off to the side.

"You down with this, Bria?" I whispered. "You don't have to go there."

"Sure, baby. Let's do this. I'm cool," she cooed, placing her arms around my neck.

"I don't want you having regrets tomorrow. As crazy as your ass is, I do value our friendship," I told her.

"Actually, this was my idea," Bria confessed. "I always wanted to know what you were working with and why you have all these girls on campus losing their damn minds over your high yellow self."

"Okay. If you're cool with it, so am I," I said with no more hesitation. It was on and popping. "Ladies, follow me," I directed, placing my arms around each of their waists, leading them to the bedroom.

It was the best birthday present ever. We worked it out through the early morning hours, taking a few breaks in between to catch our breaths and regroup. We drifted sound asleep in my bed around the break of dawn. The last thing I remember before I passed out was Tiffany and Bria taking turns sucking my dick and kissing each other in between seductive moans.

When I woke up the next afternoon, with a killer hangover, Tiffany and Bria were ghost. For a moment I thought I had dreamt the entire night and it was all a figment of my imagination, but then I saw a note attached to Tiffany's abandoned black thong. It read: Thanks for a wild night. Wow! Amazing! Damn, the rumors are true. We must do it again real soon. Happy birthday, Christopher.

When Brenden arrived later that day, I was still cheesing and reliving the night over and over again in my mind. The next time I saw Bria, she didn't say a word, acted like it never happened. All the things I did to her body, which had her moaning, squirming, cursing, and coming, and she didn't mention a damn word. Neither did I. It was our little secret. And you know what? Even though Tiffany and I hooked up several times after that before I tired of her, it never, ever happened again with Bria and me. It became our dirty little incestuous secret.

Chapter 22

Baldwin

Somehow, I made it through the moving home-going service and graveside burial. We all did. It was agony seeing them lower the light pink steel casket, overflowing with roses, into the ground. More tears spilled, bursting forth, and only Brenden's strong arms around my shoulders gave me the comfort and strength I needed to keep from collapsing. The group felt bad earlier, but the reality of the service brought the loss fully home. I think we experienced guilt. Guilt that we weren't better friends, that we didn't keep in touch, that Rihanna died without ever knowing how much she meant to each of us. Guilt was a beast.

Listening to the various tributes, hearing the preacher speak highly of Rihanna, talking to her family and friends back at her house, this all brought home loud and clear what a treasure we had and lost.

The activities of the day finally wound down. Back at the house, we attempted to put the kitchen and living room back in order as the last of the crowd gave their condolences and left. We learned many had made donations to the National Breast Cancer Foundation in Rihanna's memory. She would have appreciated that gesture.

"Whew. Look at all this food. This can feed an army for days!" Mrs. Brown exclaimed, picking up a half full casserole dish. "I know Rihanna would be upset if she was here, because this would totally blow her diet."

I laughed. I thought it might have been my first time that day.

"My daughter loved food, loved to eat. I think before she became ill, she had finally accepted her body as it was."

I nodded and remained quiet as she handed me a paper plate from the table to discard in the large green trash can that sat in the corner.

"I used to tell her all the time that she was perfect just like she was. God doesn't want everyone to be skinny minnies, because that would be downright boring. Our family produces big-boned women. It's just a fact."

Mrs. Brown handed a large white plastic pasta bowl to Bria, who was at the sink, washing dishes in sudsy water. We had slipped into jeans and sweatshirts to do the dirty work, and it was a great distraction for both of us, because keeping busy didn't give one time to think.

"I remember one time, I was sitting by her bedside at the hospital, one of her last times there, and she said, 'Mama, at least one good thing came out of my cancer.' I looked at her oddly because I couldn't imagine what. 'Do you know what it is?' she asked. 'No, baby. What?' I asked, stroking her thin hand. 'I got my wish. I'm finally skinny. All those diets I suffered through and all I needed was to get cancer.' We just laughed and laughed until we cried." She looked off into the distance, remembering the poignant moment.

"Lord, I am going to miss my baby. I don't know what I will do without her. She was my personal sunshine. Give me strength, Lord!" she exclaimed, raising her hands toward the heavens. "My baby's gone."

I swiftly closed the distance between us and gave her a big, lingering hug. I felt her entire body trembling. I didn't let go until she did.

"It's going to be all right, Mrs. Brown. I'm so, so sorry. Just pray, and I'll keep you in my prayers. We all will."

Bria stared at us, still standing silently in front of sink. She had stopped washing dishes, and she had a look of panic on her face like she didn't know what to do, like she would flee at any moment. I had noticed she had been unusually quiet since returning to the house.

"Bria, are you okay?" I asked.

Silence was her response.

"Bria?"

She slowly nodded, never making eye contact.

"Mrs. Brown, why don't you go home? Bria and I can finish up here, and Brenden and Christopher have started stacking the folding chairs for pickup tomorrow."

"Are you sure?" she asked, hesitating.

"Yes, absolutely positive. We can take care of the rest of this. And besides, we are almost finished."

"I would like to lie down for a while. I didn't realize how tired I was until now. I just want to get in my bed and sleep," said Mrs. Brown.

"We understand. Do you have anyone to stay with you? If not, I would be happy to come over," I told her.

"No, child. You stay here with your friends. My best friend, Patty, should be home by now. You probably don't remember all the people you've seen come and go today, but you met her earlier. She left to drop off some of this food and take people home. She's been living with me since she moved back from Virginia a couple of months ago. Been a godsend."

"That's good. At least you're not alone," I said, gently rubbing her back.

"I left plenty of food in the refrigerator, so y'all shouldn't have to worry about cooking anything for the remainder of your stay. Just warm it up and you're set."

"We'll be fine," Bria said, suddenly coming alive. "Don't worry about us. Thank you so much for everything. And again, my condolences go out to you and your family."

"It means so much that y'all are here for our family during this trying time," Mrs. Brown said.

"We wouldn't have had it any other way," I said.

"Seeing you here reminds me of Rihanna and happier times."

We nodded.

"I'm sorry the reading of the will won't be until Friday, but that was the earliest the attorney could schedule. I know you have to stay an extra day, but hopefully it won't be too much of an inconvenience or burden."

"Of course not. That's fine. Go home and get some rest," Bria said softly.

"I'll call you young people tomorrow and check on y'all."

"Okay," we said at the same time.

"Try to get some sleep," I added.

Mrs. Brown proceeded to gather her worn black purse and coat from the coat closet, and we walked over to give her final hugs as she opened the front door.

She turned and offered a weak smile. She looked defeated at that moment. "I know your parents are proud of you. Y'all have grown into beautiful, accomplished women, and I want you to know Rihanna loved you."

Just at that moment, Christopher and Brenden stepped back inside the house. Like us, they had changed into jeans, hoodies, and sneakers. They looked from us back to Mrs. Brown, not sure if they were interrupting a moment.

"Fellows, I'm leaving now. Like I told the girls, there's plenty of food in the fridge, make yourselves at home, and I'll check in on y'all sometime tomorrow," she said, hugging each in turn.

"Drive safely," Christopher said, kissing her on the cheek.

"Call us if you need us," Brenden said, pulling her into a hug.

"You don't know how much this means to me that you young people came to my baby's funeral. I guess Rihanna had her reunion, after all," she said with a sad smile on her face. "I know she is looking down from heaven, simply cheesing."

When Mrs. Brown quietly closed the front door behind her, we continued to stand where we were, comforted by each other's presence. I looked at Bria and squeezed her hand. Her reaction when Mrs. Brown was crying worried me, but Brenden and Christopher showing up prevented me from asking about it. I didn't want to bring it up in front of them. I guess it would have to wait until later, when we were alone.

Chapter 23

Bria

You should always leave loved ones with loving words. It may be the last time you see them.

If I didn't take away anything else from these past few days, I'd learned that we have to hold our loved ones close. True friendship, true love, those were rare. Sometimes they were a once-in-a-lifetime event.

Lying on the queen-sized bed on my back, next to Baldwin, I stared at the ceiling, had been for the last thirty minutes. I silently counted white sheep in my head. As tired as I was both mentally and physically, my eyes wouldn't cooperate and simply close. I was too wound up. I recalled that Baldwin was the opposite; during times of crisis she slept. She slept like the dead. Like she was doing now.

I glanced over at her. She was what most men would consider pretty, and she had her share of admirers back in school, but she only had eyes for Brenden. That I knew for a fact. I thought back to another time, another place, when Baldwin was going through another crisis and I was there to console and comfort her.

Baldwin had slept most of the weekend. Deep, fretful sleep.

"Baldwin," I whispered, softly calling out her name as I entered the small room, which was cloaked in to-

tal darkness, shadows prancing around in the obscure corners.

No response.

"Baldwin," I said, a bit louder this time, gently shaking her shoulder.

She stirred beneath the covers. Moaned and cried out even in sleep.

"Baldwin."

"Huh?"

"Baldwin, you need to get up and grab something to eat."

"I'm not hungry," she said in a raspy, barely audible whisper.

"Sweetie, you have to eat," I coaxed. "You are going to get sick. I walked all the way over to your favorite restaurant to bring you back chicken noodle soup."

More silence followed.

"It's a large cup," I said, hovering over her, hoping the delicious aroma would encourage her to rise and shine.

When she lowered the covers from her face, she looked an absolute mess. Her eyes were red rimmed and swollen from the crying she had been doing the past couple of days. She'd even cried in her sleep. Her hair was knotted and matted down on her head.

"I simply want to be left alone. Why can't anyone understand that? Leave me alone."

"We love you, Baldwin, and we hate seeing you like this. It breaks my heart, sweetie."

"Bria, my heart aches so badly. You just don't know, wouldn't understand. How could he do this to me?"

I sat down on the edge of the bed. "I know, sweetie, but you'll survive this. You are strong, and believe it or not, your life isn't over. It's just beginning."

"It feels like it is."

"Well, it's not. You have your entire future ahead of you."

"I trusted him, and I believed him when he said he would never hurt me."

"Baldwin, we'll get past this predicament. You and me—together."

"Will I? I don't think I'll ever be the same."

Baldwin glared at me like I held all the answers to her problems. Little did she know that I was going through my own inner conflict. I hid my turmoil inside, away from prying, accusing eyes.

"Sit up, sweetie. Just long enough to eat this. Then you can go back to sleep if you want to. Okay?"

Baldwin slowly rose to a sitting position. She looked so fragile in her pink and white pajamas. I helped her prop up the pillow and handed her the steaming cup of soup and plastic spoon.

"Be careful. It's hot," I said, handing her a couple of napkins.

"You didn't have to do this, you know."

"I didn't have to, but I wanted to. You are my best friend," I said genuinely. I could feel her pain as it pulsated from her pores, reaching out to pull me under.

Baldwin stopped eating and looked down, on the verge of tears again.

"Regardless of what you think, you are not alone in this. I realize he hurt you, but the hurt will subside. You're a survivor, Baldwin, and personally I think you made the right decision, if there is any consolation in my opinion."

Her eyes reflected an uncertainty I'd never witnessed before. Baldwin was always sure of herself.

"I can't believe he made such a fool of me," she said, shaking her head from side to side as if to clear the thought away.

"He's hurting too, believe it or not. . . ."

"He could have fooled me. He didn't have to walk in that cold, sterile place and make a decision that will affect the rest of his life, and he let me go alone. That's unforgivable."

I didn't say anything. I wanted to say I was there, but didn't want to upset her any more than she already was. I loved both of them and could see both sides. For the first time ever, the group was divided.

"Eat," I demanded, fluffing up the pillow behind her back.

"What time is it?" she asked, looking toward the window that ran the length of a wall.

"It's almost five o'clock, but do you even know what day it is?"

"Saturday? No. Sunday?"

"It's Sunday, and you've been in that bed since Thursday at noon."

"Hmmm, this is good," she said, blowing on the soup and taking another big spoonful.

"You must be starving. You only took a couple of bites of your burger on Saturday. Why don't you take a shower and change clothes, because to be honest, you stank, girl."

Baldwin looked at me and formed a hint of a smile for the first time in days.

"What? Yeah, I said you stank." I actually saw a small flicker of happiness in her eyes, and I felt my heart tug.

She smelled under each armpit and frowned. "You're right. I am kind of ripe."

"That's one way of putting it," I kidded.

Baldwin finished her soup, ate it all, even consumed a few saltines, and to my surprise, she climbed out of bed and went into the bathroom and showered.

She came back into our dorm room dressed in black sweatpants and a gray and blue wife beater. Her hair was pulled back into a messy ponytail with a scrunchie.

We sat around for the remainder of the evening, talking. We didn't talk about anything in particular. I felt that Baldwin thought if she stopped talking, she wouldn't be able to deal with her new reality. To this day, I didn't think I had felt as close to anyone as I did to her that evening.

Baldwin and I sat side by side on her bed, shoulders touching. Feet dangling over the edge. In the dark.

Out of nowhere she turned and said, "Thank you, Bria, for having my back and for being here. You'll never know what this means to me. I love you, Bria. I really do."

I didn't say anything. I felt that lurch of my heart-strings again, and she didn't turn away. Baldwin continued to stare at me with those big, hurt-filled eyes, which threatened to overflow with fresh tears.

Before I realized what I was doing, I leaned over and kissed her. Kissed her full on the lips, and to my surprise, Baldwin reciprocated. Featherlight and warm, our tongues touched and explored as we clung to each other, but it didn't last long, even though it felt like an eternity. Within a few minutes, we pulled apart, reluctant to look at one another. Breathing rushed. There was an awkward moment of silence. I guess we were trying to figure out what had just happened between us. I broke the spell.

"Baldwin, I'm sorry. I didn't mean—"

She waved me away with a weak flicker of her wrist, our eyes still not meeting.

"You were in so much pain, and I didn't know what else to do."

"Bria, don't explain."

I started to speak again.

"Don't, okay? Just drop it. Thanks again for the soup. You're so thoughtful and sweet. I don't know what I'd do without you."

"You're welcome."

"I think I'm going to lie back down."

"Okay. Sure."

"And, Bria, I meant what I said earlier. I love you. You are the sister I never had."

"I know, and I love you too."

A few minutes later, after getting up to use the bathroom, Baldwin was knocked out in another self-imposed slumber. I watched her sleep for a few minutes from my bed with the matching comforter across from hers. Then I quietly left and went for a walk across campus to clear my head.

That happened ten years ago, and here I was, still struggling with my sexual identity in some ways. Looking back, I enjoyed the sweet kiss I shared with Baldwin, and I relished the threesome I shared with Christopher and Tiffany, more because of the intimate time spent with Tiffany. I had been secretly attracted to her the first time I saw her on the yard. Just like Christopher, I thought she was sexy.

However, I couldn't admit that to myself, let alone the group, not in a million years. That was the secret I carried as I struggled with my own internal turmoil back then. I was afraid to acknowledge it to myself, terrified of placing a label on it, but I knew what I was. I had known for quite a while but thought I could outrun who and what I was. I now knew that never worked for very long. I wasn't happy, but I was good at pretending. I was good at smiling, good at being a friend, good at partying and having fun, and good at sexing random guys. I was everything to everybody, but myself.

Now the thought of telling the group that I'm a lesbian terrified me. I still was not sure how I was going to bring it up, or if I would at all. Sure, I had accepted my sexuality a few years ago, and Terry was the love of my life, but that didn't make coming out to the group any less difficult. So between the funeral and my pending announcement, I was an emotional wreck.

Chapter 24

Christopher

After Mrs. Brown's departure, we didn't know what to do with ourselves. We treaded lightly around one another, careful not to shred the final ties that held us together and prevented us from breaking down. Baldwin and Bria eventually ventured upstairs and took naps in the bedroom they shared. That left Brenden and me to our own devices.

Brenden and I hung out in the living room, alternating between making small talk, watching TV, and eating leftovers. It took me back to our college days. We really didn't know how good we had it back then. We studied hard during the week and partied even harder on the weekends and usually spent Sundays in front of a TV, watching the sports channel and drinking.

"Hey, man, you all right over there?" Brenden asked, glancing my way.

I was stretched out on the sofa with my right hand covering my forehead.

"Yeah, man. I've been better, but I'm cool."

"Just thought I'd ask, since you're pretty quiet over there."

"Just thinking. Still can't believe she's gone," I said, more to myself.

"Me neither, man."

"Why Rihanna? She couldn't hurt a fly. Man, I could almost see it if something happened to me. All the dirt I've done in the past, it would seem like payback, like karma catching up with me, but not Rihanna. It just doesn't seem fair. Makes you ask God why."

"Christopher, haven't you learned by now that life isn't fair?" Brenden volunteered. "There's no trying to figure out why things happen as they do. They simply do."

I sighed. "I guess you're right, but it's still a hard pill to swallow."

"If life were fair, I'd be happily married to Baldwin, with two babies and a house in the suburbs."

I didn't comment. I could only imagine how he felt every time he looked at Baldwin and realized what he had missed out on. Baldwin was pretty special.

"I can't believe I'm separated from my wife, can't see my son on a daily basis. And the love of my life, the one I let walk away, hates me. My life is in shambles, and I feel like there is nothing I can do about it."

"It didn't look that way in church today."

"What are you talking about?" Brenden asked.

"The way the two of you were hugged up, it didn't look like Baldwin hated you."

"Baldwin needed someone to get her through the funeral service, and I was there."

"Try to talk to her alone again," Christopher suggested.

"It didn't exactly work out the first time I tried that."

I laughed. "She is feisty, isn't she?"

"Always was. That hasn't changed."

Around eight o'clock the girls drifted downstairs in their pajamas and thick thermal socks. Bria had on a head scarf with a red, blue, and orange pattern.

It's like a funeral up in this joint," Bria declared, plopping down on top of my outstretched legs.

"Damn, Bria! It's not like you weigh ninety pounds anymore," I said, pulling my legs from beneath her.

"Owww," Brenden shouted, biting down on his hand and trying not to laugh.

"So what are you trying to say, Christopher?" Bria asked. "I'm listening. Do share."

"Nothing, Wild Child. Only that I love you," I said in my most sincere voice.

Bria gave her signature "Fuck you" look, which I had almost forgotten about. "As I was saying, Rihanna would not want us to be walking around depressed with sour faces."

We knew it was the truth, but it was easier said than done.

"Look at us," Bria said. "We look like we have lost our best friend."

"Well, we have," Baldwin piped in. "We have lost our best friend."

Bria rolled her eyes. "You know what I mean. It's a figure of speech. I know this sounds crazy, but I had a weird dream upstairs. Rihanna came to me, and she was healthy and happy. She had a beautiful smile on her face, and she told me to tell you guys to celebrate her life, not mourn it."

We didn't doubt the dream for a minute, because we had all experienced her spirit at one point or another in the past few days.

"Christopher, turn on some music," Baldwin said. "I'll get the wineglasses. Bria, grab the wine and beer."

And just like that, we celebrated Rihanna.

"Let's dance, Christopher," Bria said, reaching for my hand. "Let's see if you still have some moves."

"Oh yeah, I got your moves," I said, snapping my fingers and breaking out a dance from back in the day. "Remember the Carlton?"

Bria reciprocated.

"That's all you got for me, Bria? Come on now. You can do better than that," I teased, breaking into the Jiggy.

"Go, Bria. Go, Christopher. Go, go, go," Baldwin chanted.

Bria attempted to have a dance off as we did various dance moves from our younger days. The Tootsie Roll, the Butterfly, and Da Dip all made appearances.

Baldwin and Brenden sat on the sofa, cracking up.

"You guys are still hilarious," Brenden shouted over the music.

"Rihanna would love this, all of us together again," Baldwin said.

"Here's to Rihanna," Brenden declared, clinking his beer can to Baldwin's wineglass and then rising to do the same to me and Bria.

"Boy, if you don't stop stepping on my feet!" Bria screamed a few minutes later, attempting to walk away.

"Come back here, girl," I said, jerking Bria back onto the makeshift dance floor we had created by pushing the coffee table back toward the door.

That night we danced and drank and acted like complete fools. At some point, I exited the makeshift dance floor to grab more beer. I opened one for myself, passed one to Bria, and then collapsed on the love seat next to her, with my head in her lap.

"I'm old," I moaned.

"I tried to tell you," Bria joked, massaging my head.

A slow jam came on.

"That's my song!" Bria screamed.

"They are *all* your songs." I laughed. "Which one isn't?"

"Would you like to dance?" I heard Brenden ask Baldwin. To my surprise, she didn't turn him down cold.

They slowly walked the short distance hand in hand and wrapped their arms around one another. Bria and I looked at each other and then back at them, lapsing into silence for the first time that night.

I swear to you, at that exact moment I sensed Rihanna's spirit in the room. The group was back together again, and it seemed right. It felt good.

Rihanna beamed down from heaven.

We stayed up most of the night, drinking, laughing, and reminiscing about our carefree college days. We drank until the early morning hours, tried to drink our pain away. With the sun making its appearance on the horizon, we one by one finally made our way upstairs to welcome sleep. We were too tired for any old demons to haunt us. Booze kept them at bay. For now.

Chapter 25

Baldwin

No matter how bad your heart is broken, the world doesn't stop for your grief.

When I woke up the next morning from our night of celebration, my first thought was of Brenden. For once not of Rihanna, but of my first love. I relished the quietness and peacefulness of the house, with Bria still asleep beside me. I could think and tried to gather my thoughts. I sensed my heart was thawing out, wasn't as ice cold when it came to Brenden. Sometimes I wondered if I could have handled things differently back then, but there is no redo button in life. We can't simply turn back the hands of time and do it over with a satisfactory outcome. That day, that moment in time, still lived vividly in my mind.

"I'm pregnant!" I simply blurted it out without ceremony. I was standing in the middle of Brenden's bedroom at the apartment he and Christopher shared.

"You're what?" he asked, with an expression on his face that was hard to place at that moment.

"I'm pregnant," I repeated, unable and unwilling to meet his eyes.

"But how?"

I tossed him a look that let him know his question was absurd.

"You know what I mean. You're on the pill."

I shrugged my shoulders. "It isn't one hundred percent effective, and remember the time I spent the night and forgot to take it?"

Brenden nodded. His face still held a look of shock and disbelief.

"Say something, Brenden. I can't take your silence much longer."

"How long have you known?" he asked.

"Not long. A few weeks. I wanted to be sure."

"I'm sorry," Brenden said, closing the distance between us, pulling me into his strong, muscular arms. "We'll get through this the same as we have gotten through everything else we've encountered."

"Yes, I will. First thing Monday morning, I'm scheduling an appointment at the clinic."

"What clinic? What are you talking about, Baldwin?" he asked, his voice rising an octave.

"The abortion clinic," I said, softly lowering my eyes to the floor.

"You can't possibly be serious," he said, suddenly releasing me and stepping back two steps so he could look into my face. "Answer me," he demanded. "Are you serious?"

I flinched at his tone. "I'm very serious. There aren't any other options, Brenden."

"Damn. Unbelievable. You come in here, tell me we are about to become parents, and then in your next breath state you are going to kill our baby."

"What do you want me to do?" I shouted, finally looking at him.

"Keep it. Raise it. Love it. We are about to graduate. We can make it work. We aren't the first and won't be the last to have a baby."

"That's easy for you to say. You don't even have a job lined up yet. Neither do I. Keep it? You are so naive, Brenden. I know you want to save the world, wipe out racism, poverty, and homelessness, but you can't fix this. This you can't," I shrieked, shaking my head.

"Why not? I love you. I thought you loved me, Baldwin."

I was frozen to my spot in the middle of his bedroom. My body started to shake uncontrollably, but Brenden stayed rooted to his position and made no effort to console me.

"I do, baby," I said in a near whisper.

"You do what? Love me? Or want to kill my unborn child?" he questioned.

"I do love you."

"You have an interesting way of showing it."

"Why are you making this so difficult for me?" I questioned. "It doesn't have to be," I said in a calming tone. I finally got the strength to move toward him, place my arms around his neck, and pull him close.

"See? There's your answer, Baldwin. It's always about you. What you want. What about what I want? Have you thought about that for even a second?" he asked, slowly removing my arms and placing them at my sides.

I remained silent, trying to hold back tears, which slowly inched down my cheeks. I had promised myself I wouldn't cry.

"Answer me. What about me? Did you even think about me in your fucking decision, Baldwin?"

"I don't want to be a statistic, another unmarried woman with a baby. Do you realize how difficult a baby will make my life, our life? I didn't spend four years out of my life to attend college and then graduate to change diapers."

"Who's to say we won't get married? You know I'll be there for you," he said, pacing back and forth now.

I didn't respond.

"Damn, I can't believe you had the audacity to walk your ass up in here to tell me some bogus shit like this. What kind of woman are you? Do you have a heart?"

I started to sob at that point, softly at first. "I thought you knew. I'm still the woman you love. Nothing has changed, baby. I'm just not ready for such a huge lifelong commitment. Why can't you understand that and accept it?"

"You! You! You! That's all you can ever think about. That and what other people will think of you. Get over it, Baldwin. Stop caring about what other people think or feel or say about you. At the end of the day, they don't matter. Only you and I do. We are in this together, and I thought you understood that."

"I can't do it! I just can't! I'm sorry," I cried, burying my head in my hands. Instead of comforting me, Brenden moved to the opposite side of the room.

"One question. So you are absolutely going through with it?"

I nodded, slowly meeting his stare.

"Without my permission?" His eyes shot daggers my way, and my heart sank.

"I don't need your permission. This is my body and my decision," I blurted out.

"When you lay down with me and spread your legs, that united us. What's growing inside you is part of my seed. It's just as much a part of me as you," Brenden said in a quivering voice.

"I'm sorry, Brenden. I really am. Please don't hate me, but I have to do this. And I'm going to."

Brenden backed down, looked like he was going to cry any second, tried to compose himself, and when he looked back up at me, all I saw was disgust reflected in his eyes.

"Get out! Get the fuck out!"

I froze, didn't dare move.

"Did you not hear me? Go! Get the fuck out of my apartment, Baldwin!" he shouted, grabbing me by the arm and literally dragging me out. "I can't deal with this."

"You'll change your mind once you've had a chance to think through this. It's for the best, and I need you to go with me to the clinic," I screamed out.

"Are you serious?" he asked, stopping at the front door and opening it.

I remained quiet, because I was afraid to answer. I had never seen him like this.

"Since it is your decision and it's all about you, go by your damn self. I sincerely hope you can continue to live with yourself after it's over, after you have killed our baby. You are not the woman I thought you were."

"Brenden! Please!"

He silently opened the door wider. He didn't or couldn't even look at me. I felt lower than low. I opened my mouth to say something, but he wouldn't hear it. I realized he had shut me out of his heart.

"Bye, Baldwin. Go, please!" he screamed, looking over my head.

When I stepped outside seconds later, he literally slammed the door in my face.

From that point on, for the first time, the group was divided. Everybody chose sides while trying not to. Bria supported my decision, and Rihanna chose to side with Brenden. And I instantly suffered a deep sense of betrayal from her since she was a woman and should have understood my position. Christopher stuck in the middle, tried to play both ends. However, that never worked. You couldn't play both sides. Your loyalties always lay in one place or another. Eventually they showed themselves for what they truly were.

Chapter 26

Brenden

It isn't enough to be forgiven by others. Sometimes you have to learn to forgive yourself.

"Aren't you glad I talked you into coming along for a walk?" I asked.

Thursday had brought a somewhat sunny, crisp winter day. During the afternoon the temperature was perfect for a stroll in the woods and a trip back down memory lane.

"It is beautiful out here," Baldwin agreed, glancing around at the foliage as we slowly made our way along the narrow nature trail. We weren't in a rush. "I bet Rihanna loved this. She was such a nature lover."

"You're beautiful," I volunteered, unable to stop myself from saying it out loud. I believe Baldwin actually blushed.

"Thank you."

"You always were, but the years have made you even lovelier."

"Stop, Brenden. Save it for your wife," she said, with a hint of anger suddenly cropping up.

"Baldwin, to be honest, I won't be married much longer. I've come to the realization that my marriage is over. Actually, I think I've known for a while. I need to stop fooling myself. There's no fixing it, and Rihanna's death has made me realize that life is too short not to be happy."

Baldwin didn't comment. She simply continued to stroll along the path we had discovered in the woods behind Rihanna's house. Her arms were folded stiffly across her chest.

"No comment?" I asked, attempting to catch her eye. Her body language said it all.

"You're correct. None at all. I have no interest in your personal decisions, nor would I expect you to have any in mine. Not anymore."

"Ouch. That was cold."

"Whatever, Brenden. I'm just keeping it real, but I realize the truth does hurt."

"Honestly, why are we doing this?" I asked, throwing up my hands in complete surrender.

"Doing what?" she asked, abruptly stopping to glare at me.

"Arguing. I'm sick of us going at each other. We are supposed to be enjoying our afternoon walk together, embracing nature at its finest."

"I agree." She attempted a smile, assuming her leisurely pace once more. "You're right."

"What? We actually agree on something? The world must be coming to an end."

She smiled, and my world felt brighter.

"I've missed you, Baldwin."

She suddenly stopped in mid-stride, her eyes and body language letting me know she had retreated, as she always did when she was uncomfortable.

"What's wrong?"

"There you go again. Maybe this wasn't such a good idea, after all. I think I'm going to walk back to the house."

I gently grabbed her hand, because I didn't want to scare her away. "Please. Don't go. Not yet."

"Let go of me," she said nervously, recoiling as if I had burnt her with my touch.

"Damn, are you going to spend your entire life running from me, Baldwin?"

"I'm not running!"

"You could have fooled me. I don't bite, Baldwin. I just want to get off my chest what I've wanted to tell you for a long time."

"I've never stopped you," she said, regaining her composure.

"Baldwin, who isn't being real now? Who are you kidding? I tried numerous times over the years, even right after graduation, to reach you, to apologize. You always ran like I was the fucking black plague."

"There wasn't anything left to say, then or now. You didn't want me. You made your choice and moved on. End of fucking story."

"Is that what you've thought all these years?"

She looked at me in disbelief. "Yes. Actions really do speak louder than words in my book, so what was the point in talking?"

Baldwin and I continued to walk slowly, with our shoulders touching.

"Damn, so much happened back then. Our relationship was complicated, and we were incapable of dealing with it. We were too young."

"Yet you wanted me to bring a baby into the world when we weren't even grown up ourselves?" Baldwin asked.

"Yes, I did, because it was our baby. I loved you so much back then, and I couldn't for the life of me believe you had even halfway considered terminating the product of our union."

To my surprise, my voice started quivering and all the pent-up anger, frustration, sadness, and remorse came bursting forth. Full force. I scared myself with the passion that I possessed.

"I realized it would have taken a great commitment on our part, but I was very willing and able to do just that, Baldwin."

"Excuse me if I'm wrong, but you proved that by screwing another woman and getting her pregnant? And not just any skank, but the one who had been trying to get with you since freshman year, regardless of the fact that you and I were together!"

"You hurt me. Can't you understand that? I'm a man, but I'm not too proud to admit that you hurt my heart. Malia offered hers, and I accepted."

"That you did. You eagerly accepted and didn't waste any time replacing me."

Suddenly I felt my anger rising to an even higher level.

"Don't forget that your shit stank too, because your slate wasn't exactly sparkling clean, either. Let's not forget your little indiscretion."

Baldwin quickly turned away as we came to a clearing with a small creek.

"Baldwin, you shouldn't throw stones when you live in a glass house yourself. The two people that I loved the most betrayed me."

Baldwin's shoulders started to visibly shake, and she slowly sank on the mossy ground, hugging her knees. There were tears glistening in her eyes as I dropped to the ground beside her.

"I'm sorry, Brenden. I didn't mean to hurt you. I really didn't. I was young and scared, and I didn't know what else to do. At the time, it seemed like the only logical option I had. If I had it to do over again, would I make the same decision? I honestly can't say. Forgive me so that I can forgive myself. Do you know how many times I have looked at a child, a stranger in the streets, and thought that our child would have been around that age? Or how many times I've wondered how our baby would have looked? Guilt is my constant companion every day of my life."

"Baldwin, I forgave you a long time ago and acknowledged my role in everything. So please stop beating up yourself."

She nodded and exhaled. "As for the other part, what went down, I regretted it afterward. But he was there and familiar and comforting."

I lowered my head and tightly closed my eyes for a few seconds. "Thank you. I've been waiting ten years for an explanation, and I want you to know that I didn't mean to turn my back on you. I was angry, and I pulled away. I didn't know how to deal with my pain back then. If I could take it all back, I honestly would."

"I believe you, Brenden. It's all in the past, so let's move on. Forgive and forget."

I continued purging my soul. "Then Malia got pregnant, and I thought it was a sign that God was giving me a second chance for a baby and a family."

"Is that why you married her?" she asked quietly.

I picked up a rock that lay at my feet and threw it in the small creek; small waves rippled outward, breaking the stillness that existed before. I watched until the last wave disappeared.

I heaved a sigh. "I've thought about the answer to that exact question many times over the years, and I honestly don't know. I don't know if I was trying to get back at you or if I thought I could grow to love her since she was giving me something you refused to."

Baldwin didn't blink, stared straight ahead.

"But you know what?" I asked.

"What?"

"She couldn't replace you. I never did grow to love her like she wanted me to because you still had my heart. That never changed. As much as I tried to fight it, I couldn't forget you."

She smiled a sad smile that didn't quite make it to her eyes. She whispered, "You don't know how many times I thought of you over the years. I always compared my boyfriends to you, and none of them ever came close. They never measured up."

Minutes passed in silence. We were digesting all that had been said, words that should have been spoken years ago.

"Answer just one question for me. Was part of what you and he did out of spite on your part?" I questioned.

"It just happened," she said, looking at me with shimmering, sorrowful eyes.

"Classic line that means nothing, Baldwin."

She tried to look back down. Wanted to avoid my stare and judgment.

I gently raised her chin with my hand, made her look at me. "I guess it doesn't matter. I figured he was exactly what you needed at that time. I wasn't blind. I knew he was attracted to you but tried hard to hide it. We always covet what we can't have. I figured if he could provide you an ounce of comfort when I couldn't, so be it. So I forgave him."

Chapter 27

Baldwin

Back then, I didn't have anyone I could turn to. Brenden wouldn't have anything to do with me. He made me invisible. He wouldn't talk to me, wouldn't even look at me if we crossed paths on campus. Bria was there but was too caught up in her own drama to give 100 percent support. Rihanna had very traditional, conservative views regarding abortion. Soon I started to keep my distance from her because I couldn't handle what I saw as her accusing, judgmental eyes. So eventually, I found myself drawn to one of the closest persons to Brenden.

I knocked, timidly at first, then louder. Three heavy taps. I heard steady, firm footsteps and stood back until he opened the door.

"Hey," he said.

"Hey, yourself," I said, shifting from foot to foot. Suddenly I felt nervous and unsure of myself.

"You look like hell."

"Thanks a lot. I feel like it too. Is he here? I didn't see his car outside," I said, trying to peer inside.

"No, he went home for the weekend. Come on in," he said, opening the door wider as I stepped around him.

I walked in and sat on the tattered hand-me-down brown sofa. The tears started to flow almost instantly; I absently swiped at them. He was suddenly quiet, and I noticed the mood quickly shifted. I realized my crying made him uncomfortable and he had never seen me cry.

"I'm sorry. I didn't know where else to go. I hope you don't mind," I said, looking up at him anxiously. I wouldn't have been able to bear it if he turned me away.

"Not at all. You know I'm here for you. You my girl, Baldwin." He still hadn't sat down.

"I know this places you in an awkward position. I'll leave if you want me to."

"Like I said, I'm here for you. You are always welcome here."

"Thank you, Christopher. That means a lot."

He ever so slowly approached the sofa, staring at me with genuine concern as he took a seat next to me.

"How are you holding up?" he asked.

"Okay, I guess. I've been better. That's for sure." I attempted a laugh, which came out as something else.

"Listen, baby girl, I want you to know that I'm behind you one hundred percent. I know this isn't an easy decision for you."

"Regardless of what Brenden and Rihanna think, it isn't. I'm scheduled for next Friday."

He nodded. "I sympathize with Brenden's point of view, but what does Rihanna have to do with any of this?"

"She doesn't mean any harm, but she is all up in the mix, talking about how she doesn't believe in abortion and how the Bible explains it is a sin. Telling me how I'm terminating a life. Informing me about the adoption process, which she has researched online, and how we should consider that."

"Rihanna means well."

"I guess, but I don't need to hear that shit. I just need her support. And Bria has appointed herself my personal nurse maid when she isn't in the streets."

Christopher laughed. "That's our wild child, and we know how Brenden has reacted."

"Yeah, he hooked up with Malia," I said, my voice cracking at the mere thought.

"You've got to understand men, baby girl. He's hurt, and she's throwing it at him left and right. The man is weak and vulnerable right now."

"Oh, you support his actions?"

"No, I'm not saying that. He'll come to his senses sooner or later."

"What if he does and doesn't want me, or maybe I won't want him?"

I started crying again. This time loud sobs filled our space. Christopher seemed uncomfortable once again.

"I'm sorry, Christopher. I didn't mean to bring my problems to your doorstep." I sniffed between sobs.

"That's what friends are for. It'll all work out, I promise you."

I had my head on Christopher's shoulder, and he gave my back circular strokes as my sniffles slowly subsided.

"You think so?" I choked out.

"My mama is always saying, 'This too shall pass.' It may look bleak at the moment, but you'll survive, and so will Brenden."

"I feel like such a fool."

"You shouldn't feel that way. Hold your head up. You're simply making the right choice for you at this moment."

I wiped the last of my tears away with the back of my hand. "Since when did you become the voice of reason?" I managed a weak chuckle. "This is new."

"Brenden's a fool, and I've told him so. He doesn't realize what he has in you."

"Thank you. I really needed to hear that, Christopher." I turned, looked at him shyly, our eyes met, and it just happened. We started kissing and touching, timidly at first and then more frantically.

He stopped first. Pulled away. "No, Baldwin. We shouldn't. This isn't right."

"Please, Christopher. I need you," I cried, with my face burrowed in his neck.

"Are you sure about this?" he asked.

I nodded. "I need to feel wanted and safe."

"We can't take this back, Baldwin. Never."

"I don't see Brenden worried about me. He's too busy in the arms of another woman."

Christopher nodded and bent down beside me on the floor as he slowly undressed me like I was a fragile doll and then laid me back on the sofa. The air was thick with raw emotion.

"You are so lovely," he murmured.

I reached up and stroked his face, with tears in my eyes.

"Don't cry, Baldwin. I hate to see you upset."

"My Christopher, you've been such a supportive friend. I don't know what I'd do without you. I know it hasn't been easy for you, either."

"I'd do anything for you, Baldwin. Anything to make you happy. I mean that."

In that instant, I believed him and I wanted to be with him more than anything.

Christopher slowly undressed, and his eyes never left mine. His eyes projected all the lust, joy, and longing he had held back for so long. I looked away, couldn't stand to see the truth that I had always tried to block out. I'd known. I'd always known.

He climbed on top of me, showering me with hot, passionate kisses. He was ever so gentle. Treated me like I would break if he didn't touch me with love. When our bodies touched, skin to skin, I felt my problems drifting away, at least for that moment. Christopher was exactly what I needed, exactly what the doctor ordered.

"How could he—"

"Shhh. You're with me now. Just close your eyes and think happy thoughts. I would never hurt you. Ever."

I did just that. When Christopher slipped inside me, he felt so good, and for the first time in days, I felt loved.

"You look like an angel," he whispered.

I opened my mouth and a deep moan escaped as he gently nibbled on my neck.

"I want to make you forget all the bad. I'll always be here for you, baby girl. Just relax," he said, stroking long, deeply, and tenderly.

With that I was lost in desire. He spread my legs wider with his knees, kissed every inch of my body, and proceeded to make love to me in a slow, deliberate manner. He filled me up. When it was over, I was extremely satisfied, and I knew we had bonded on another level that could never be broken. At the same time, we immediately realized what a mistake we had made.

I started to cry again, and he simply held me in his arms. He didn't say a word, simply stroked my face. I fell asleep on his chest, with him silently consoling me. We had moved a blanket onto the floor. A few hours later I stirred from my position and quietly got up. Trying not to wake Christopher, I silently pulled my clothes back on, which were scattered on the floor, near the sofa. However, he was already awake by the time I was dressed.

"You don't have to go, you know. You can wait until the morning. We can get in the bed so you'll be more comfortable, or you can take my bed and I'll crash on the sofa."

"No, I really need to get back to the dorm," I said, not able to look at him now.

Christopher rose from the floor, still nude. I averted my eyes. Now I was too ashamed to look at what had hours ago given me so much pleasure.

He slowly lifted my chin so I would look at him.

"Baldwin, what we did wasn't wrong. Promise me you won't beat up on yourself. If you want to assign blame to someone, place it on me. I took advantage of your emotional state. Okay?"

"Okay," was all I could muster.

He quickly dressed in sweatpants and a T-shirt.

"You good?"

I nodded.

"You sure?"

I nodded again.

"Baldwin, I meant every word I said, and making love to you meant something special to me."

"I know you did, but you know my reality."

"I do, and I respect that. I have no other choice, do I?"

"I'd better leave," I said, walking toward the front door.

He didn't try to talk me out of it this time.

"Thank you, Christopher. For being here for me."

"Let me drive you back to the dorm."

"You don't have to."

"I want to, and I am going to."

Christopher and I rode in complete silence, both of us lost in deep thought. Both of us knowing what a mistake we had made and how we could never take it back. *When we arrived at my dorm, I eagerly opened the passenger door to get away from my mistake.*

"Wait, Baldwin."

I slowly turned to face him.

"I know how this—"

"You don't have to explain. I wanted to. I needed you. Don't worry. This will stay between you and me."

Christopher relaxed at my words, and the obvious tension left his shoulders.

"I'll talk to you later," I said, realizing I probably wouldn't before the words left my mouth.

"See you later."

"Yeah."

Christopher and I made a vow of secrecy, but eventually everything had a way of coming to light. Brenden discovered the truth. The group was pulled further apart, and nothing would ever be the same.

Chapter 28

Christopher

Bria was talking nonstop as usual, chatting about random thoughts that came to mind. We were driving into Raleigh to check out some of our old haunts. Much had changed, yet her company felt comfortable and familiar. Like coming home. I hadn't felt like sitting around the house all day. I was antsy.

"Too bad Baldwin and Brenden didn't ride out with us," she said.

"I think they needed some alone time."

"You sure about that? We might get back and find out they've torn the place apart." She laughed. "Those two mix like oil and water now. A huge departure from back in the day."

I didn't comment one way or the other. "Hey, remember that club that catered to college students we used to hang out at? What was it called?" I asked, changing the subject.

"The Warehouse," we both said in unison.

"That was the spot, but this area has really changed since we were college students," I said.

"What did you expect? We've been out of school for ten years. Nothing remains the same. Life goes on, man."

"True. Can you believe ten years has flown by so quickly?" I asked.

"Nope. It seems like just yesterday we were young, impressionable college students with our entire lives ahead of us."

"You are doing exactly what you said you would do. Taking the fashion world by storm. You're successful," I chimed in.

"I wouldn't exactly say I'm taking it by storm, but I am in my field . . . doing what I dreamt of doing, only on a smaller scale."

"I'm proud of you."

Bria glanced at me. "Look at you. All grown up and dishing out compliments."

"I *am* proud of you. Plus, I'm glad you found someone and settled down."

Bria shifted in her seat and suddenly looked slightly uncomfortable. She cleared her throat a couple of times and fidgeted in her seat some more.

"You look happy," I said.

"I am," she agreed. "Very happy."

Bria and I drove along in silence for a few minutes. I was taking in the sights, noting the changes in my surroundings. I had enjoyed four years of fun and freedom in this city, like I never experienced afterward. This was my first opportunity to really see it in years. When I used to visit Rihanna, we never went anywhere, always stayed close to home and in bed.

"What's the deal with you?" Bria questioned.

"What do you mean?" I asked.

"You said you met this woman, you're ready to commit, but there's hesitation on her end."

"My reputation precedes me."

"It always did," Bria said with a straight face.

"Give me a break. Anyway, I've hurt her in the past, and now she doesn't trust me as far as she can throw me. I can't say that I blame her, but I really have changed."

"Don't give up on her. If you are using the L word, then it must be real. She's the one."

"Me?" Look at you, all glossy eyed and emotional over your man. Used to be Miss Fuck 'Em and Leave 'Em."

"Was I really that bad?"

"Yes," I said with no hesitation.

We laughed, comfortable in each other's presence.

"You know what? I'm not ashamed of a minute of it, because I was finding myself," she observed.

"And lots of dick."

Bria turned to give me a mean stare.

"Bria, I'm just kidding with you. You weren't doing anything most dudes on campus weren't doing. Why should I look down on you because you are a chick?"

"Very liberated thinking."

"I try."

"Remember when you and I hooked up for a night?" she asked out of the clear blue, watching for my reaction.

"Of course. How could I forget? That's one of my fondest college memories," I said. "I still have wet dreams about that night." I laughed.

"Do you think the group ever knew?"

"No, I doubt it. I think we got that one past them."

"Good for us. I like that we share one secret among ourselves," she said and winked. "What do you think about Baldwin and Brenden? I just knew they'd be together forever."

"Shit happens. Rihanna's death is a prime example," I replied.

Bria nodded. "True, but it was like they were meant to be together. You remember how they were on campus. Inseparable. You saw one, you saw the other."

"Times of stress can pull people apart and break bonds," I volunteered.

"Christopher, just say it! Everybody has been skirting around the truth this entire couple of days. Dirty little secrets. After Brenden knocked Bria up, she had an abortion right off the bat, Rihanna became a Bible-toting fanatic, Brenden started fucking that bitch and knocked her up, and then the kicker. You fucked Baldwin, your best friend's woman. Now, that's more than a little stress. That's some major shit."

I didn't say anything. Bria had summed it up in a nutshell.

"Simply scandalous!" she screamed.

"That's when the dynamics of the group started changing . . . us pulling away from each other."

"Do you regret it?" she asked.

"What?"

"Sleeping with Baldwin?"

I didn't hesitate. "No, I don't. I gave her what she needed at the time."

"Yeah, you broke her off some."

"No, I gave her comfort, listened, and made her feel good in the process."

"I bet you did."

"Bria, you are sick. Be serious for once, please."

"Okay, seriously, at first I passed judgment. I'm going to admit it. But after Baldwin broke it down, I understood. It was less about the sex and more about the comfort. If Brenden can forgive you . . . well, actually his shit stank too. He fucked that bitch and then got caught up with her drama. I still say she got pregnant on purpose. Trapped him. She wanted his ass the first day she saw him on the yard, and everybody knew it."

"When you break it down like this, we were worse than any of these reality shows on TV."

Bria nodded. "There was never a dull moment, that's for sure. When I look back, I don't know how in the hell we graduated."

I laughed.

"Do you want to stop somewhere for lunch?" Bria asked. "Because I'm starving. Plus, I can't take any more collards, chicken, or casserole dishes."

"Cool. You choose," I said.

We rode in silence for the next few miles, and my mind wandered.

I recalled the door slamming so hard, it sounded like an explosion vibrating throughout the apartment, shaking the paper-thin walls. I was walking out of the bathroom. It was a Friday night. I rounded the corner and took a right square in the jaw. It was on right from the start.

"You fucked her!"

"Fucked who?" I asked, trying to buy time and remain calm.

"Don't give me that bullshit, you bastard! You know exactly who I'm talking about!"

Brenden was furious; I had never seen him like that before. He was all red-faced and breathing hard, like he had run for five miles nonstop. His nostrils were flared and his fists balled, in attack mode.

"Man, how could you? I never expected you to do anything like this to me. I thought we were boys. Partners. Then you sneak behind my back and screw my woman?"

"Correction. She wasn't your woman anymore." My temper started to boil over too.

"Go to hell! You've been sniffing behind Baldwin since you first met her. Jealous as hell that she was with me and not interested in your egotistical, womanizing ass. She just wanted to be your friend, and that deflated that gigantic ego of yours."

"You don't know what you're talking about," I shouted, taken aback for a second.

By now, we were in the living room, pacing back and forth, eyes not leaving one another.

"Man, I've always known you were in love with Baldwin. I'm neither blind nor stupid. I've seen the way you've watched her, looked at her, when you thought she wasn't looking. I knew. It burns you up that she hooked up with me, of all people. Doesn't it?"

I couldn't say anything, because Brenden was on point with most of what he had said. It was true. I loved Baldwin, and she was everything I had ever wanted in a woman. I backed away, still rubbing my tender jaw. If it were anyone but Brenden, the campus police would have to break up the whipping I'd put on his punk ass.

"Admit it!" he yelled.

"I'm not admitting shit, man."

"How could you go up in my woman? Biding your time all these years, just waiting for the opportunity for me to fuck up."

"How could you not see how much pain she was in? Still is. Did you think it was easy for her to have an abortion? And you and Rihanna all up in her face, making her feel like some sort of monster. Damn, man! The woman loves you."

Brenden's shoulders slumped, and he slowly sat down on the sofa, with his head buried in his hands.

I went on. *"What about Baldwin? You let her go through that shit all by herself, and in the meantime, you screw her rival? And Bria has to go with her to that fucking clinic."*

Brenden started to speak, but just as quickly closed his mouth.

"What exactly does that say about you, man?" I scolded. "Baldwin is supposed to be your woman, and you talk about how much you love her. According to you, she's your soul mate. Then you turn around and abandon her during her time of need, embarrass her by sleeping with some slut, and then you have the audacity to step to me! Man, get the fuck out of my face! You're a joke."

I was pacing back and forth again. I was now the one who was furious and spewing forth my venom.

I continued. "Yeah, I admit it, if that will make you happy. I slept with Baldwin, but it wasn't what you think. It wasn't dirty or calculated like you think. I don't know how to describe it. At her lowest, she came to me, and I gave her what she needed most, not sex, but a connection, some understanding, and comfort. Did you offer up any of that?"

Brenden slowly shook his head.

"I didn't think so."

"You're absolutely right," was all he said as he stood up, walked into his bedroom, and slammed the door so hard that a cheap framed print fell off the wall, with glass shattering to the floor.

Brenden and I successfully avoided each other for the next few weeks. Luckily, I had a couple of evening classes, and he was a morning person. Brenden and I came and went like complete strangers without getting in each other's way. It was weird living with the person I thought I had betrayed, especially after word traveled around campus and the gossip mill took off.

I found myself wondering about what he had said, trying to deny the truth in his words. Had I really wanted him to fuck up so I could make my move? I didn't know. I didn't think so. One thing was certain. Regardless of what went down between Baldwin and me, she still loved Brenden. Me, she loved as a friend. As I accepted it before, I accepted it afterward.

The damage was done; the group was torn. Things had been said and done that could never be taken back. We could never go back to what we were before.

The group didn't even realize that the shit still hadn't hit the fan full force. Eventually, Brenden and I apologized to one another, shook hands, and graduated as friends, just not as close. If roles had been reversed, I didn't honesty know if I would have been able to find it in my heart to forgive him if he had slept with my woman. However, I really believed if I had it to do all over again, I would have done the exact same thing. Baldwin needed me.

Chapter 29

Bria

"We're here. Earth to Christopher."

"Huh?"

"Dude, what's up with you today?" I asked, pulling into the restaurant parking lot.

"Nothing. I'm cool."

"You could have fooled me," I said. "Are burgers okay with you?"

"Sure. A juicy burger and a cold beer or two sound great."

"You didn't get enough drinking in last night?"

"Never," he joked. "You know how we used to do it."

"Yeah, we'd get white boy wasted. Where were you?" I asked, pointing to his head.

"I was thinking back to our college days. We really were thicker than thieves, and then we graduated and nada."

I shook my head in confusion. "We have a lot of baggage, man."

"That's one way of looking at it."

"I always said we were our own little dysfunctional family. We needed therapy."

I pulled into a parking space not too far from the entrance to the restaurant, which looked like it was on its last leg.

"This place has the biggest, juiciest burgers in town," I assured him. "It's not much to look at from the outside, but trust me. You'll love the food. I've been here a few times over the years."

I was still contemplating how I was going to reveal my secret. It was important to me that the group knew the life I now led. If they rejected me, so be it. It was time to come out, out of the closet to my friends, to finally reveal my identity.

Ten minutes later Christopher and I were seated in a booth near one of the many dingy windows in the restaurant. The waiter had left to fill our orders after dropping off two foaming beers in frosted mugs.

I sipped and licked the frothy foam from my lips. Christopher and I were sitting facing one another.

"Do you think they are going to do the do?" I asked.

"Who?"

"Adam and Eve. Duh. Who else? Baldwin and Brenden."

Christopher shrugged his shoulders, uninterested, and drank his beer, looking around at our surroundings. "Bria, you need to stay out of their business."

"I think they still love each other. Baldwin would never admit it, but it's written all over Brenden's face. I just want them to have their happy ending. The one they should have had years ago."

"My hope is that if nothing else, they resolve all their issues. You can't go through life with regrets, resentments, and misgivings," Christopher said.

"I agree."

"Life is too short," he said.

Chapter 30

Brenden

Arms linked, Baldwin and I continued our nature stroll, enjoying each other's company.

"That's the one thing I could never understand," Baldwin said.

"What is that?" I asked.

"You were able to forgive Christopher back then, but never me."

"Even though he was my partner and slept with you, I felt you delivered the ultimate blow."

"And you were innocent in the entire situation?" she asked, dropping her arm.

"I never said that. Listen, I thought we were going to place that all behind us and start fresh?" I said, nudging her shoulder.

"You're right, Brenden." She smiled. A beautiful, genuine smile that set my heart on fire. "Today, this second, is a new beginning."

"So change the subject and talk about something else."

"I can tell you enjoy being a father," she said, reaching for my hand.

"I do. I absolutely love it. I can honestly say I love that little boy with all my heart and soul. Do you think you'll have children someday?"

"Hopefully, someday. I'd like that, because I feel I'm ready to be a mom."

"What's the wait?"

"Well, silly, I have to find a husband first."

"I thought you were dating Mr. I Love You, Baby from the phone the other night."

"I am, but . . ."

"There's that word. But what?"

"I'm not sure he's the one."

I had to force myself not to smile at that declaration. "At least you're being honest and not rushing into a situation simply for the sake of being married. I speak from experience, trust me. Marriage is no joke and a lot of hard work."

"Look at me. I let you talk me into taking a walk, and now I'm telling you all my personal business." Baldwin smiled again, and her eyes lit up, sparkling.

I stopped in mid-step.

"What?" she said when she caught me staring.

"You are breathtaking."

She blushed. "There you go. You're embarrassing me again."

"Well, you are, and I've missed you."

I slowly leaned toward her and lifted her chin. I was almost afraid to touch her, because this was the moment I had dreamt of and I couldn't believe it was actually happening. We kissed. Slowly and deliberately. We took our time in rediscovering each other. I wanted to savor the moment and memorize it for my long, lonely nights.

"Nice." As we pulled apart, I couldn't stop grinning like I had won the million-dollar lottery.

"Uh-huh," she murmured. "I think we should go back."

"Why? It's still early, and I enjoy being with you."

"I just think we should go back."

"Sure, if you want to," I said reluctantly.

On the walk back, Baldwin talked about everything but us. She brought up crazy stuff the group had done that I had almost forgotten, like playing drinking games, Truth or Dare, and going into grocery stores and turning the sample food items into our lunch on the weekends when we were all broke. Those were the days. To be young and free again.

Our walk was exactly what the doctor ordered. With just the verbal admission of forgiveness, I felt like a one-hundred-pound weight had been lifted from my shoulders. My step was lighter. I also realized I had never gotten over Baldwin, and I was definitely still in love with her.

I had always tried to live my life with no regrets, because we couldn't change the past. What was done was done. There wasn't any going back, only moving through it, but sometimes I wondered how my life would have been if Baldwin and I had married and had children.

I knew for sure it was over with Malia. We were legally separated, anyway, had been for over six months. At one point I had considered trying to work it out for my son's sake, but I now realized I had never felt an ounce of love for her that I felt for Baldwin.

Later that evening the group was back under the same roof. Bria talked nonstop about her and Christopher's adventure. They had dropped by old haunts, had stopped for lunch, and had gone to the local mall. And they had made another beer and wine stop.

After pizza delivery from a local restaurant, we called a time-out and checked in with our significant others.

Calls were made; texts and e-mails were answered. After that it was on, and we partied the rest of the night away. Like it was 1999. Like before, the group had the music blasting from a station that played eighties and nineties music and the drinks flowing. We once again pulled back the coffee table and danced until we wore ourselves out with our bad moves and laughter.

Bria found some old photo albums, and as we flipped through the pages, we were transported back in time. Rihanna had captured so many moments of our college years. Each new page brought forth old memories. Many times I'd glance up to find Baldwin staring at me, and she'd look down when our eyes met. She looked lovely with her bare feet curled up underneath her as she sat near Christopher. I could still smell her perfume that lingered on my skin from earlier that day.

Later, much later, Baldwin and I danced to a few slow tunes. We were close, touching, remembering. She felt so good in my arms that I didn't want to let her go.

"Can I be with you tonight?" I whispered seductively in her ear.

She paused but didn't pull away as I'd expected. "Excuse me?" she finally whispered back.

"I want to make love to you."

"I don't think so."

"I know you are still attracted to me. Admit it," I kidded.

"You're married."

"Technically, yes. Remember, I'm legally separated."

"I'm in a relationship, Brenden."

"Baldwin, you have already admitted that you aren't sure where it's going."

"Hush. Just dance. Just hold me," she said, leaning her body seductively into mine.

I did just that. I held on for life and meshed with her.

As the night wound down, along with our energy levels, we knew the next day would hold surprises and answers to all our questions, such as why were we included in the will? What would be Rihanna's last words to us?

The group climbed the stairs a little after one o'clock with the realization that this was our last night together. The next day, after the reading of the will, we'd all go our separate ways. Possibly forever. That brought great sadness my way, especially when I thought about Baldwin. I didn't want to lose her again. Not twice. That would be unbearable.

Chapter 31

Baldwin

In a determined state of mind, I found myself quietly and carefully sneaking out of the queen-size bed I shared with Bria, careful not to wake her. Then I eased my way across the hallway to Brenden's room. In my thin white gown and with no slippers on, I silently inched my way through the blackness that surrounded me, holding on to the walls to guide my path. I asked myself with each step I took, *What am I doing?*

My question remained unanswered, and my resolve to get to Brenden was unrelenting. I stepped into his open doorway and stood there, in the shadows, soaking him up with my eyes, watching him sleep silently. Just as I remembered, his face was calm and peaceful. Brenden always slept like he didn't have a care in the world. I smiled as emotion pulled at my heartstrings and wetness seeped between my thighs.

As if sensing my presence on some innate level, Brenden slowly opened his eyes and peered directly at me. I froze. Our eyes met, and in the silence and calmness of the moment, we knew what the other needed and wanted. Brenden slid swiftly from beneath the covers, walked over to me in three quick steps, took my hand, and gently closed and locked the bedroom door. He led me back to his bed, and we were in our own private space for the first time in ten years. My heartbeat, along with my breathing, sped up. My mouth went dry.

When his lips meet mine, Brenden literally took my breath away. In that instant, I realized that was what I had longed for, for so many years. To be in his arms again. To feel his desire and boundless love. We both sensed it as our spirits reconnected and reunited. A missing part of me was being made whole again. I would never forget that moment. Ever.

"Brenden?" I said, looking up at him, with multiple questions reflected in my unsure eyes.

"Don't say anything," he instructed, pressing his finger gently to my lips. "Go with this moment that has been presented to us, Baldwin."

I gazed at him, stared deep within his soul, and realized I wanted to be with him more than anything in the world at that moment. Brenden proceeded to slip off my flimsy cotton gown and panties with not much effort as I anxiously lifted up my hips to assist. I lay back and watched as he pulled down his black boxers and stepped out of them, leaving them on the floor. I wasn't afraid or nervous or uncomfortable. This was our moment, our destiny. It was where I belonged, with Brenden. When he climbed back into the bed and on top of me, I exhaled long and deep.

Brenden softly and gently kissed and caressed my neck and face with such passion and tenderness. "I will never hurt you again, Baldwin. I never stopped loving you, not for a second."

My passion was rising like floodwaters at a steady and even pace. Heat and desire overtook my body at a level I had never experienced before. My entire body was on fire. I was burning up. I couldn't think straight. I didn't want to. I was caught up in being intoxicated with our lust. In a state of lovesick bliss was exactly where I wanted to be.

"I've missed you too," I moaned in his right ear as my tongue encircled it.

Brenden and I held on tighter to one another. We were afraid that if we let go, we'd lose each other again. As he slowly eased himself down and lovingly sucked and stroked my tender breasts, I lost my breath and closed my eyes and savored the intense pleasure. His finger, then two more, slipped inside my wetness, and I almost lost my mind.

"Ahhh, baby, you feel good," he grunted.

"Don't ever stop what you're doing to me," I moaned in a whispery, seductive tone as I applied pressure on his hand to push his fingers in deeper.

I trembled as his hands spread my legs apart and he ever so gently eased himself inside. Expanding. Taking his time, learning my body all over again. Slowly he filled me up to the brim and started to rock slowly, at a steady pace.

"Damn, I've missed this. Only you take me above and beyond," Brenden said.

My fingers dug unmercifully into his shoulders with each upward stroke.

"Right there, baby. Oh, yesss," I gasped.

"Does that feel good?"

"Ahhh, yesss."

"I just want to please you, baby."

Brenden thrust deeper, and I almost passed out with desire. He was all up in my womanhood, making me feel each stroke.

"Have you missed us?" he whispered in my ear.

"I have," I cooed breathlessly.

"Show me, then," he whispered in a low, deep, guttural voice that turned me on even more.

I slowly started to grind back into him as he eagerly pushed my legs back to meet my chest.

"Ahhh, oh, Baldwin," he groaned huskily in my ear.

Our moans and groans were soon drowned out as he greedily took my tongue into his mouth. He slowly inched in and out, deeper and harder, grinding as he caressed my breasts with both hands and stared lustfully into my eyes. All too quickly, I felt the familiar rising tide of an orgasm coming on and coming on strong. As I rode the waves of ecstasy, I started to moan and I threw my head back with my eyes tightly closed.

Brenden stopped. "Baldwin. Look at me."

He started his rhythm back up once I reopened my eyes. In and out. Out and in.

"I want to know the exact moment you come," he said, still into his delicious groove between my legs. In so deep that I couldn't tell where he began and I ended.

Brenden tweaked my nipples with his thumb, and I groaned even louder as I scratched his back with my fingertips. When I felt myself going to my pleasure peak, I let out a loud half wail, half scream. With several deeper, delicious thrusts, he joined me in our own private pleasure trip to ecstasy.

Before the sun rose, we made love two more times. Each time was better than the last. We couldn't seem to get enough as our hands and mouths explored, relearned. Completely exhausted, we fell asleep snuggled in each other's arms, and shortly before six o'clock I managed to rise and sneak back into my bed, with Bria none the wiser.

Chapter 32

Bria

Glancing at Baldwin sleeping soundly like a baby, I literally rolled out of bed. I couldn't sleep the night before, so I was wide awake. I had tossed and turned most of the night, so I was very much aware of Baldwin sneaking into Brenden's room. She had been hilarious, and it had taken everything in me not to burst into laughter.

Right now that was not the most important thing on my mind; it came in at a close second, though. I was fully aware that today was the day. I wouldn't get another chance. It was now or never. Today was the group's last day together, and I had to reveal my secret. The problem was that I was as nervous as hell and hadn't quite figured out how I'd tell them that I was gay.

I had played out the scenario in my mind several times over the past few days. Sometimes I simply blurted it out. Other times I would call them together and tell them I needed to talk with them about a serious topic. I even entertained the idea of telling them individually or maybe even e-mailing the news. Bottom line, however I told them, I didn't want the group's opinion of me to change. I was still Bria. I didn't want to be judged or treated any differently. I was pretty sure that wouldn't happen, but I had found that people would surprise you when their idea of what was right and wrong was challenged. I stumbled into a hot shower with those thoughts heavy on my mind.

Two hours later, the group was assembled downstairs, eating the last of breakfast, which I had been more than pleased to fix as they showered, dressed, and packed upstairs. Cooking scrambled eggs, bacon, and pancakes had given me something to do, and it was an attempt to keep my mind off of my pending announcement. I had decided I was going to tell them at breakfast, and the last two hours I had been a nervous wreck. I had come out to everyone else in my life that was important to me. Some took it well; others didn't. So Baldwin, Brenden, and Christopher were the last to hear my news.

I kept myself busy as they ate, cleaning up the mess I had made in the kitchen and refilling their plates with second helpings. When they were finished, I took a seat at the table. It was my moment of truth.

"Thanks, Bria. That hit the spot," Christopher said with a warm smile, taking his empty plate to the sink.

Baldwin and Brenden nodded. They had been giving each other secret stares and smiles throughout most of breakfast, as if Christopher and I didn't notice. I decided to mess with them and put off telling my secret a bit longer.

"How did everybody sleep last night?" I asked, looking at Baldwin and then Brenden.

"I think I was out before my head hit the pillow," Christopher volunteered. "I'm getting too old to party like we did back in the day."

"How about you, Baldwin?" I asked.

"Fine," she said.

"You're mighty quiet over there. What about you, Brenden?" I said.

"No complaints on my end, either. I slept like a baby."

"I bet you did," I said, with a smirk on my lips and an all-knowing look. "Baldwin, when I got up this morning you were snoring," I teased.

"Bria, I was not. I don't snore. Never have."

"You were this morning. Maybe something wore you out." I mused.

"I guess all the events of the past few days have finally caught up with me," Baldwin shared.

"I woke up during the night, looked over at you, and you were nowhere to be seen," I revealed.

"Oh, I, I, uh, I was probably in the bathroom," Baldwin stuttered.

"Oh, that's where you were?" I couldn't contain myself any longer and burst into laughter, along with Christopher, who had been trying to contain his outburst behind a closed fist over his mouth. "Baldwin and Brenden, who do y'all think you're fooling? I know what went down last night."

"Who wouldn't know? The neighbors a mile away probably know. All that moaning and groaning and screaming," Christopher said. "I woke up and thought I was in a zoo or on an African safari. Damn, I thought you were killing each other up in there."

Baldwin covered her face with her hands. She was totally embarrassed. I believe she was actually blushing. Brenden simply grinned like the cat that caught the canary. Busted.

"I'm happy for you guys. I really am. Personally, I always thought you belonged together," I said.

Christopher raised his orange juice glass. "A toast to new beginnings and lifelong friendships."

"Cheers," we proclaimed in unison.

"What time did Mrs. Brown say she was coming by so we can trail her to the attorney's office?" Brenden asked.

"We still have a little time, about an hour or so," I answered.

"Cool," Brenden said, rising from his seat at the table. "Thank you, Bria. Breakfast was right on time."

I cleared my throat, because I knew it was time to confess. "Uh, Brenden, wait." He turned to look at me.

"I, uh, I . . ." Now I had piqued their interest. All three were staring at me, waiting for me to complete my sentence. I was rarely at a loss for words.

"Bria, is something wrong?" Baldwin asked, looking at me expectantly.

I closed my eyes for a few seconds, took two deep breaths as I hid my hands underneath the table so they wouldn't see them shaking uncontrollably. "No, not at all." I couldn't do it. I couldn't confess. "I just wanted to say that I will miss you guys so much."

"Same here, Bria," Brenden said, giving me a curious look. Everyone started to get up. "But this isn't the end. We'll keep in touch."

I silently repeated to myself, *I can do this. I can do this. I can do this.*

"Uh, wait. I really need to speak with you guys," I said with a bit of nervousness in my voice.

Three sets of eyes suddenly turned and focused on me at the same time.

Breathe, breathe, breathe.

I blurted it out before I lost my nerve. "I'm a lesbian. And I don't live with a boyfriend, but with Terry, my girlfriend, the love of my life, the best thing that has ever happened to me. That's who I am, not who you think."

There. I had said it; I owned it. Now I waited for their reactions, and I wasn't sure what they would be. For the life of me, I couldn't read the expressions on their faces. I couldn't tell if they were shocked, surprised, or disgusted. Again, I had seen the worst come out in people, my mother included. If they rejected me, I would be hurt to the core. That I knew. The group had once known me better than anyone in the world, and I loved these people. I respected their thoughts and opinions. It was important to me that they accepted me. I knew it shouldn't matter, but it did. I held my breath in anticipation.

"Okay, cool. That's great," Christopher was the first to blurt out. "Anything else you need to share?"

Brenden and Baldwin nodded, with unreadable expressions.

"I guess I need to finish packing," Brenden said nonchalantly.

"Me too. When we leave, we won't be back," Baldwin said.

"Did you guys hear what I said?" I questioned, a bit too loud, looking at each of them in turn for a response.

"Yes," Baldwin said. "We did."

"Well?"

"Well what?" Brenden chimed in.

I shrugged my shoulders, confused.

"Bria, haven't you figured it out yet? We love you. We don't care who you choose to love as long as you are happy. That's the bottom line. As long as she makes you happy, makes you glow like you are, then we are happy. Are we surprised? Yes. But this weekend has been chock-full of surprises," Christopher said, walking to my side.

"I agree with Christopher," Baldwin said. "As long as you are happy, then we are too. This doesn't change anything. Being a lesbian isn't who you are. It's what you are. You are still our crazy wild child." She came over to give me a big hug and a kiss on the cheek.

"Bria, thanks for sharing. I'm sure this wasn't easy for you, but we have your back regardless. That is never going to change," Brenden said, joining the circle that had suddenly surrounded me in an embrace. "We love you the person."

Fifteen minutes later I sprinted upstairs, locked myself in the bathroom, sat on the closed toilet lid, and cried like a baby. My soul was at peace. A huge weight had been lifted from my shoulders, and most importantly of all, my friends had given me the greatest gift of all, unconditional love and acceptance.

Chapter 33

Baldwin

I was sitting on the edge of the bed upstairs, desiring a few minutes of solitude before it was time to leave, trying to sort out everything that had occurred the past few days. Now, this latest development had my head spinning. Wow, Bria was a lesbian. Now, that was a shocker, but just like I told her downstairs, it didn't change anything. She was our Bria, and I could care less about who she chose to love as long as she was happy. I was sure it wasn't easy for her to come out to us. In fact, it took a lot of courage. I assumed many questions would come later, but for now and always, she would have my full support.

"Hey, you guys, Mrs. Brown is pulling up outside," Bria screamed, leaving the kitchen, looking out the bay window from the dining area. Our plan was to trail Rihanna's mother to the attorney's office and then come back to the house to say our final good-byes.

"Here I come," I shouted from the top of the stairs, attempting to bring my suitcase down.

"Let me help you with that," Brenden said, coming up behind me and effortlessly carrying my bag down the narrow steps. We smiled shyly at one another before breaking eye contact. Brenden and I had been doing that a lot that morning, smiling. Grinning for no reason at all, completely out of the blue.

"Let's get this show on the road," Christopher chimed in, opening the front door before we made our exit.

As we closed and locked the front door, waved at Rihanna's mother, and climbed into Brenden's car, I suddenly felt strange. Weird. The funeral was one thing, we'd made it through that, but to hear Rihanna's final words and thoughts was quite another story. I broke the silence that had taken up temporary residence in the car. The vibe was suddenly tense.

"What do you guys think Rihanna could have possibly left us, and why? I mean, it's not like we've been her best friends in recent years. Ten years have passed with little contact."

"I don't know, but I guess we'll soon find out," Christopher said from up front with Brenden.

"That we will," Bria confirmed.

Brenden simply kept his eyes on the road, wore a serious expression, and didn't respond either way. He concentrated on his driving.

The law offices of Rickman, Taylor, Miller, & Smith, attorneys at law, were located on the fourth floor of a brick building that from the outside was very formal, traditional, and impressive. We quietly accompanied Mrs. Brown up on the elevator to the office suite, all huddled together like baby ducks being led to water for the first time.

We entered the fairly large conference room, following the instructions from the friendly receptionist at the front desk. Seated behind a large table with leather chairs on each side was a jovial older man, attorney Rickman, who wore a charming, easy smile. He rose and greeted Mrs. Brown, offered his condolences, introduced himself, and welcomed each of us in turn with a firm handshake.

"I'm pleased y'all could make it today. I'm sure the deceased, Miss Brown, would be satisfied as well since she included y'all in her will and thought very highly of each of you."

We nodded, smiled weakly, and took seats on the same side of the table, unwilling to separate. Once again, Bria and I sat between Brenden and Christopher, enclosed in a layer of protection. Rickman sat at the head of the table, and Mrs. Brown sat at the other end, facing him.

"Okay, let's get started," the attorney said, placing a manila folder that contained important-looking documents in front of him. "I'm sure y'all are anxious. Just know that's normal. Relax."

Mrs. Brown stared straight ahead, not displaying any emotion on her face. She was brave and dignified with her salt-and-pepper hair.

"It's my understanding that these young people need to catch planes to return to their perspective cities and homes, so at the request of Mrs. Brown, I'm going to skip the beginning of the will and focus on what was written for each of you. Since y'all have been so accommodating in this matter, from my understanding, extending your stay, I wouldn't want you to miss your flights."

He picked up a document and started reading. "This is the last will and testament of Rihanna Ann Brown. Witnessed and signed with her being of sound mind and memory. Which of you is Christopher Bivins?" Attorney Rickman asked.

Christopher reluctantly raised his right hand. At that moment, I didn't think he trusted himself to speak. I thought my heart was going to jump out of my chest, and the attorney hadn't even called my name. The attorney paused briefly and then continued in his professional tone and efficient manner.

"Okay, very good. We'll start with you, then, Mr. Bivins. This is a letter Rihanna Brown penned and would like for you to keep. She requested that it be read to the entire group, and of course, you will receive the original copy." The letter read:

Dearest Christopher,

If you are reading this, then I've gone on to glory. Don't be sad or shed any tears for me. I lived my life, and I lived it the best I could, with all I had. I'm in a much better place now. I'm whole, I'm happy, and I'm at peace. So you should be happy for me.

I'm not going to make this long and complicated. There are just a few words I'd like to say. The last time I saw you, the last time we really, truly spoke without the pretentious pleasantries . . . Well, let's just say, I do not want those to be the last words you remember. Please do not feel guilty.

Christopher, I've always loved you. Loved you from the first moment I set eyes on you on campus. You were so beautiful and confident. Your charm was intoxicating to a naive girl such as myself. When I realized you didn't like me in a romantic way, I hurt for a minute, but I was almost just as happy to have you as my friend. At least I could be in your life, maybe not the way I wanted to, but I was there nevertheless. In your inner circle. I felt it was a privilege.

What I'm trying to say is that you brought much joy into my life. The time we spent together recently was priceless, and I can't be upset that I wasn't the one for you. I still love you; I probably always will—even from heaven, looking down.

*What I ask of you, Christopher, is that you find
the one that makes you happy and then be happy.
It's that simple. You'll know when you've found
her. You are a good man, Christopher. You have a
great heart, and you have much to offer the right
woman. Take care of yourself.*
Love always,
Rihanna

I didn't know if Christopher breathed throughout
the entire reading. Even though he wouldn't make eye
contact, I could still see the tears clearly gleaming. He
kept his head bowed low. Bria reached out to touch his
shoulder.

The attorney moved on, pausing for only a moment.
"Miss Bria Williams?"

Bria slowly raised her hand high.

"These are the last words addressed to you by Miss
Brown," the attorney said, then began to read.

Dear Bria,
*Remember the last time we spoke? I'm sure you
do, and I hope you have resolved your situation.
Like I told you then and as I say now, life is too
short to waste on what people say or think about
you. People are going to talk about you until the
day you die. That's just human nature. I realized that much too late. If you've found the love
of your life, don't waste another day on people
trying to sap your happiness. Go for it and never
look back. Never. Do you hear me? When it's all
said and done, we are responsible for our own
happiness. Claim yours.*
*I love you, Bria. Always have. Your adven-
turous, free-spirited nature enabled me to open*

up, be more outgoing and willing to take risks, chances, and truly experience life. Because of you, I ventured out and opened a children's clothing boutique without absolutely any experience. I asked myself, "What would Bria do?" And I knew you'd seize the opportunity and work your butt off to make it successful. That's exactly what I did.

I've learned so much from you about not holding back, not placing limitations on myself, and most of all, I've learned how not to be afraid. I don't want you to be, either.

Embrace who and what you are. Hold your head high. You're beautiful, talented, and successful. Be happy. Be happy with whoever brings that to you in turn. All the other stuff doesn't even matter. I almost realized this too late. All the extras don't even matter, girl. I love you.

Stay blessed,
Rihanna.

Each reading provided a new revelation. At this point, Bria was openly crying. Her sobs were coming from somewhere deep within, like she was releasing a part of herself. Everyone's defenses were tumbling down. The attorney slid a box of Kleenex in her direction. We were being publicly exposed and were reveling in the wonderful, wise friend we had lost. Before we could get over Rihanna's inspirational words to Bria, Attorney Rickman continued with the reading of the will. Mrs. Brown sat quietly, taking it all in. Unselfishly allowing the moment to be for us. She didn't utter a single word.

"Brenden Bailey?" the attorney asked, looking to Brenden for clarification as to who was who. "I take it that would be you?"

"That's me. I'm Brenden," he said, raising his hand like we were back in grade school. A slight smile escaped my lips.

Attorney Rickman began reading slowly.

Dearest Brenden,

I think of all the members of the group, you and I were most alike in spirit. I bonded with you immediately because you have such a warm, caring, and genuine spirit—wanting to save the world and make everything right and everyone happy, but yourself.

Brenden, my final words to you are to find your happiness. It's not as far away and untouchable as you may think. I think we both know where that happiness lies. It's not too late. It never is as long as you have breath and life in your body. We all make mistakes at some point in our lives. We're human. But I find through prayer and trying to put myself in someone else's shoes, sometimes you'll see things much differently. I've learned to simply try wearing somebody else's shoes for one day. That's all it takes.

It's been a while since you and I last spoke. You didn't realize what a pleasure it was to run into you that day. A true blessing that I will forever be grateful for.

Find your happiness, Brenden. Do you realize how rare it is to find the person who is placed on this earth just for you—your soul mate? That's rare, too uncommon to walk away from. You know what you need to do. Fight for her. You deserve every ounce of happiness you can handle.

Stay blessed, and I'll love you always,
Rihanna

I glanced at Brenden with a thick lump in my throat. I couldn't swallow as I tried to fight back the fresh tears that threatened to release themselves. I had to pour a glass of ice water from the crystal pitcher that sat in the center of the table. Brenden looked at me and reached for my trembling hand. When I stared into his eyes, I saw nothing but pure, unadulterated love reflected back. In that moment, I knew I couldn't live without him, again.

"And that leaves Baldwin Sparks," Attorney Rickman proclaimed, looking in my direction. "Are you ready for Miss Brown's final words?"

I nodded because I couldn't speak. I looked at Mrs. Brown. She had her eyes tightly closed and was repeating, "Praise, God. Praise, God. Praise, God," over and over again. Rihanna's presence was all around us in the room. I think we all experienced it and delighted in it.

The attorney began, and I swear it was as if everyone in the room magically disappeared. All I could hear were his words, Rihanna's words.

My dearest Baldwin,

I love you so much! I want to take the time while I have breath left in my body to apologize to you. I'm truly sorry! I'm sorry I wasn't there when you needed me the most. I know I let you down, and for that I will forever have guilt in my heart. You see, at that time in my life, I hadn't grown to a level of maturity. I hadn't learned that sometimes it wasn't about me and what I was feeling or what my beliefs were, but about being there for my friend in her moment of need, regardless of differences. I needed to have taken my own advice and to have tried to walk in your shoes.

Did you know I always looked up to you? Wanted to be like you? Wanted your life in some ways? I laugh now because I realize we can only be who we are meant to be. I regret that you never responded to my letter, but I understand. I feel that you're still hurting, suffering from an aching broken heart, but believe me when I say everything is going to be all right. Follow your heart; it never leads you wrong. You are levelheaded and strong willed, but you will be fine. I know that with certainty, because joy comes in the morning. We all have to live out our destinies. Go with peace, Baldwin.

Love you forever,
Rihanna

I finally was able to focus again, and I realized everyone in the room was staring at me. I saw their mouths silently moving, but I couldn't make out the words. I was too overcome with emotion. Shadows of colors splayed before my eyes, and I felt extremely hot.

"Are you okay?" Brenden asked with deep concern.

"Do you need more water?" asked Bria, reaching for the pitcher.

"Baldwin?" Christopher asked, worry lines etched on his forehead.

I smiled at the group, wiped away the tears that flowed freely now, and said, "No, I'm fine. I'm better than fine. I'm better than I've been in a long time. I'm right where I belong."

And it was true. Even though I hadn't known I was missing it, I realized I felt a sense of peace engulf me. I embraced it back.

Chapter 34

Bria

It was a little after one o'clock, and it was the moment I had dreaded all day. The final good-byes. I was never good at saying farewell, and this was no exception. We had said our farewells to Mrs. Brown, with promises not to be strangers, back at the attorney's office, and she was going to make sure we received the various photos Rihanna requested we have in her will.

The group was clustered in a semicircle on the sidewalk outside Rihanna's home. It was a beautiful, crisp day, the kind found on the front of postcards that said "Wish you were here," and I realized the people standing before me were probably the best friends I'd ever had in my lifetime. Each person had touched and transformed my life in a positive way.

With Rihanna's spirit all around us, I experienced such a deep sense of family, connection, and belonging. I think we all did. It was obvious we were not in a hurry to part ways, even though some of us had flights to catch. The past few days had taught us a lot about ourselves, and I think I spoke for all of us when I summed up the meaning of life in general.

"Bottom line. Time moves on and waits for no one. Life is short. Make the most of it and be happy," I said. "Guys, promise me here and now that we are going to keep in touch."

"It's a done deal. I have everyone's contact info in my BlackBerry," Christopher said. "Besides, we have to have another reunion that's not under such grim conditions. I'll plan it myself."

"You and that CrackBerry," I said, gently nudging him with my left shoulder. I'd miss this man, with his sexy ass. "You plan it, and I'll definitely be there with my party shoes on. Maybe you'll have some new dance moves by then." I turned. "Baldwin and Brenden. What about you two?" I asked, looking directly at them.

They were caught up in their own world, much like during our college days. There wasn't an inch of space between them. They nodded. Baldwin was actually glowing. She looked 360 degrees happier from when I picked her up at the airport just a few days ago, which seemed like a lifetime ago.

"I'm for real, you guys," I said. "People always make promises, then life happens, and you look up and another ten years have passed in the blink of an eye."

"We aren't going to let that happen this time around. Once was enough. Besides, we have to keep in touch so that we'll have the opportunity to meet your partner," Brenden said.

"And when all the dust has settled, we have a wedding to attend," Christopher said, smiling at Brenden and winking at Baldwin. "I have to prepare my best man speech."

And in that moment, I knew he sincerely meant it. He had finally gotten over Baldwin, even though he would never admit he was once in love with her. That was another unspoken group secret.

I noticed Baldwin and Brenden didn't affirm or deny his comments. I, for one, was simply thrilled with the fact that they'd found each other again. Hurt, disappointment, and regrets could be like a virus or a terminal illness eroding your life.

"I guess this is it," Baldwin said, looking around at each of us, as if committing us to memory.

"Yeah, we'd better head out of here before you guys miss your flights, and I have a long drive back to Maryland," Christopher said, but he still didn't move one inch toward his car.

"Come on. Group hug. Everybody give me a hug so I can hit the road as well," I said, my eyes suddenly tearing up. I didn't think I had cried as much as I had the past couple days since I was a child. They were cleansing tears.

The group huddled in a circle and exchanged hugs, kisses, and good-byes. It was a moment that should have been captured in time for all eternity.

"I love you guys. I'll miss you so much, and I mean that," I said. "You've given me so much this weekend, so much peace," I whispered, placing my hand over my heart.

"We love you back, Wild Child," Christopher said, giving me one last tight squeeze.

I laughed at that and said, "I got your wild child."

Gradually, we reluctantly pulled apart from one another, not wanting to break the invisible link that bound us. I noticed everyone took a last look at Rihanna's house, as if saying final good-byes to her. I could almost see her spirit smiling down on us. The past days, the mini reunion, had accomplished just what I thought she had intended. Old wounds were healed. Forgiveness was granted. Friendships were renewed. And we left with a greater appreciation for life and the ones we had in our lives, whether on a daily basis or in our hearts.

After they pulled off one by one and blew their car horns, I sat in my car for a few minutes, reflecting on everything that had happened. These past few days had made all the difference in the world, and for that I'd be forever grateful.

Chapter 35

Baldwin

"Hey, baby. I missed you in bed this morning," William said, walking up behind me to nuzzle and kiss my neck. He had spent the night with me, even though it wasn't the weekend. This was a rare occurrence.

He scared me, and I jumped. I was so lost in my personal thoughts that I hadn't heard him walk into the kitchen. As corny as it might sound, the days spent with the group were a life-changing experience. I arrived back home with the knowledge that something was missing in my life and I needed to seek out my happiness. Instead of drifting through life, I needed to live it.

"I couldn't sleep. Instead of tossing and turning and waking you up in the process, I gave up and got up," I said. "Besides, I'm off from work today. I'm taking a personal day to run some errands."

"You should have stayed in bed. You know how I love waking up to you in my arms."

"What do you want for breakfast?" I asked, ignoring his comment. I got up from the kitchen table to lean against the counter. "What do you have a taste for?"

"The usual. Two eggs, three slices of turkey bacon, and a cup of juice. You know what I like."

"Okay," I said nonchalantly.

William stopped, turned, and looked curiously back at me. "Are you okay, baby?"

"I'm fine. Why?"

"Since you returned from North Carolina, you've been acting different. You haven't been yourself."

"I haven't noticed," I said, breaking eye contact. Before the words left my mouth, I knew I was lying.

"You still haven't told me about the trip."

"You and I have been busy, and besides, what is there to tell? It was a funeral."

"We haven't been that busy, and before you left, you were anxious about going to see your long-lost friends," William said. "Now it's a nonissue?"

I hunched my shoulders. "Pretty much."

"If you say so," he replied, wearing an expression that told me he didn't believe a word I'd said. "We'll talk later."

Thankful that he didn't continue this topic, I proceeded to take the egg carton out of the refrigerator, and William walked to the bedroom to change into his running gear for his morning run. He had spent the night the night before, and I was shocked. William was such a workaholic that I rarely saw him during the workweek. We would talk several times throughout the day, and I liked it that way, because I didn't want a live-in boyfriend.

Still distracted, I removed four eggs from the carton and the bacon from the refrigerator and placed them on the kitchen counter, near the stove. William was 100 percent correct. I hadn't been myself the past couple of weeks. I had been back for two weeks, and everything was different somehow.

Even my home didn't feel right anymore, like something or someone was missing. I had talked to Brenden pretty much every night since we left North Carolina.

We would talk for hours throughout the night, and I hadn't laughed so much in my life. I always reluctantly hung up with a smile on my face and joy in my heart, and I was tired as hell the next morning, but I was ready to do it all over that night. Brenden and I caught up on the missing years when we'd had no contact. Now it felt like we hadn't missed a beat.

On the other hand, William now appeared to be making an extra effort to treat me extra special. It was almost as if he sensed I was pulling away. It didn't matter. Something was still missing. The only person who filled that void was Brenden, and he was coming to Atlanta in a few days and wanted to see me. As much as I wanted to see him, I also realized this would be a turning point.

Chapter 36

Bria

"How was your date?"

"We had a wonderful time," Baldwin said nonchalantly.

"Details, more details," I shouted into my cell phone.

"Girl, you are so nosy," Baldwin said playfully, giggling like a love-smitten teenager.

"I know I am. Now that we have that established, spill all the juicy details. Quickly. I'm dying to hear."

"You are too much. Okay, I picked Brenden up at the airport, and he was looking sexy and smelling good as usual, and I couldn't for the life of me stop smiling. Girl, I was cheesing, and I was feeling all giddy, like a teenager going out on a first date."

"Awww, how sweet. Go on."

"Brenden and I pretty much hung out near the airport since he wasn't going to be in town long, and we didn't want to waste our time together riding all over metro Atlanta in heavy traffic."

"Makes sense. What did you guys end up doing, besides screwing each other's brains out?"

"For your information, we stayed at the Hilton Airport, in separate rooms, watched a movie, and had dinner and drinks. So there."

"Wait! Hold the hell up. Did I hear you say *separate rooms?*"

"Yes, you did. Thank you very much."

"And why, may I ask? What's up with that?" I asked.

"Brenden and I decided we aren't going to rush things. His divorce isn't final. In fact, he hasn't even filed the paperwork yet, and I'm still in a relationship with William."

"That didn't stop you two in North Carolina, now did it?"

"Whatever." Baldwin chuckled.

"You know I love you like a sister," I said jokingly.

"We decided to take a step backward for a minute and not rush the physical part."

"How did you manage to get away without William getting suspicious?"

"I told him I had to attend a weekend conference for my job, and he didn't have a reason not to believe me. Besides, William had a lot of work to catch up on and had plans to work through the weekend."

"I didn't know you had it in you, bitch. Sneaky, sneaky, sneaky."

"I feel bad. I don't want to hurt William, but I really wanted to see Brenden again and spend time with him."

"I agree you shouldn't rush things, but I still say the two of you belong together and you've already wasted too much time being apart."

"I won't disagree."

"You know, you are eventually going to have to make a decision about William."

"I know. In some ways, I guess I already have."

"Just follow your heart," I suggested. "It never leads you wrong."

"What's going on with you and Terry?" Baldwin asked. "Tell her I said hello and I can't wait until you guys visit next month. I'm looking forward to it."

"Okay, I will. We couldn't be happier since I returned home after Rihanna's funeral. I've placed closure on much of the bullshit that was fucking up my life."

"Good. You deserve all the happiness you can take," she said.

"And so do you. I even reached out to my mama, and we actually talked. No screaming. I can't say it wasn't awkward, uncomfortable, and hard, but at least we are talking."

"That is wonderful, Bria. I'm so happy for you. Take one step at a time."

"Listen to this. Are you sitting down?" I asked.

"Why?" Baldwin asked. "After North Carolina, there isn't too much of anything you could tell me that would blow me away."

"Terry and I are thinking about adopting a baby girl."

"Wow. I think you'd make a great mother."

"I appreciate that coming from you, and to be honest, I'm super excited about the possibility, but right now we are just thinking about it. But let me run, girl. I just wanted to see how things went with you and Brenden."

"I'll talk to you later," Baldwin said.

"I'm off to the gym. Nowadays, I have to work on keeping this figure as fine as it is."

"Don't we all. Have fun."

"Fun isn't what I'd call it. My personal trainer is kicking my ass backward and forward. Talk to you later, girl."

"Bye, Bria."

I hung up with a smile on my face. The group had kept its promise; we were keeping in touch.

Chapter 37

Brenden

"How's ole girl?" Christopher asked.

"Who?" I asked innocently.

"Man, don't even try to go there with me. You know damn well who I'm talking about."

"Baldwin is fine," I said and laughed.

"You would know. I've heard about your frequent trips to the ATL. Hotlanta."

"I have business in Atlanta."

"That you do." He chuckled.

"Bria needs to stop gossiping all the time. Some things never change," I said.

Christopher and I laughed as friends who had history together did.

"Can I be honest with you?" I asked seriously.

"What's on your mind?" Christopher asked.

"I've fallen in love with Baldwin all over again. Not that I ever truly stopped loving her, but this time around it is a more mature, stronger love."

"Good for you. I'm happy for you, man. I've done so much dirt in my lifetime that now that I'm ready to settle down and truly commit, my lady doesn't trust me as far as she can throw me."

"Keep at it. You'll eventually wear her down. She's a beautiful woman, and when I had dinner with you guys that night, I knew she was the one. Hell, the two of you complete each other's sentences, and I didn't see those wandering eyes of yours checking out all the other women in the restaurant."

"I hope you are right about wearing her down, because believe it or not, I have changed. I've grown up. I've sowed all my wild oats, because, let's be honest, after a while it gets old."

"Tamara's simply trying to be sure you're for real and probably trying to teach you a lesson in the process."

"True that. I hope so, anyway, man, because I'm not going anywhere. What is your soon-to-be ex saying about your frequent trips to Atlanta?"

"Malia doesn't suspect anything. The few times I had to cancel plans to pick up Jordan, I told her I had to go out of town on business. Besides, it's none of her business because we are legally separated."

"Uh, you keep thinking that. I've learned to never underestimate a woman. You might think she doesn't know, but if I were you, I'd keep my eyes and ears wide open before the shit hits the fan. Unfortunately, she'll be in your life until your son turns eighteen, and whether you think it's her business or not, she can make your life a living hell."

"That wouldn't be anything new," I said in disgust. "Welcome to my world."

"Hang in there."

"I will, and you too, because I am dying to see your ass married, living in a two-story home with a basement, driving an SUV, and going to monthly PTO meetings."

"See, don't start with me, man. Don't go there. That's the part that scares the shit out of me."

"What did I say?" I asked, trying to sound innocent.

"Keep acting dumb." I laughed. "I'll hit you up later."

"Okay, dude. Peace."

Chapter 38

Baldwin

I had never been good at lying. I always went into much more detail than I normally would, and I couldn't meet the person's eyes. I had learned sooner or later that the lies always caught up with you one way or another. Unfortunately, mine was sooner.

I couldn't believe my eyes when I slowly turned onto my street and was in the process of turning into my driveway. If I had known he hadn't seen me, I would have simply kept going, but it was too late. Damn, I was caught.

"Baldwin, where in the hell have you been?" William asked, running up to my car before I could even get the gear in the park position.

Slowly opening my car door, I got out. I wasn't sure what to expect as I attempted to formulate a response in my mind.

"It is six o'clock in the fucking morning!" he screamed, only mere inches away from my face. I instantly smelled the strong aroma of liquor on his breath and knew immediately that the scenario playing out was not going to be pretty. Alcohol always made William more aggressive.

"What are y-you doing here?" I stammered, trying to push my way past him and remain calm and cool at the same time. However, he continued to block my path. "I thought you were out of town for the week, William."

"Well, I'm not. And I thought your ass would be sitting at home on a Saturday night—correction, Sunday morning—while your man was away. You fooled me."

"What are you doing? Spying on me?" I asked, taking a defensive stance with my arms crossed and perched over my breasts.

I finally managed to inch my way around him. William was still hot on my tracks as I made my way to the front door.

"No, the fucking question is, what are you doing? You look like you just crawled out of someone's bed, and it sure as hell wasn't mine."

"You've been drinking, and you're talking crazy."

"Come here! Let me see if you smell like dick!" he shouted, tugging on my arm and stopping my escape.

"You're talking crazy and drunk. Go home, William! You know I don't like it when you drink," I screamed, pulling out of his grasp.

"Where have you been, Baldwin?"

I kept walking, tried not to run to my front door, but I didn't appreciate how he was ranting and raving at me. William's behavior was starting to scare me. Suddenly, he grabbed my left arm to stop me in my tracks again.

"Answer me, Baldwin!" he screamed, swinging me around to face him.

"I was visiting a friend who was passing through town. We had drinks, dinner, and before I knew it, t-time had flown by. So I st-stayed over at the hotel," I stammered, unable to meet his angry, bloodshot eyes.

"Male or female?"

"Why? Does it matter?"

"Damn it. Male or female?"

"Male!" I screamed. Something deep inside of me wouldn't allow me to lie to William. He deserved the truth, regardless of his harsh reaction. I owed him that much, and I would have expected the same.

"Did you fuck him?"

"William, let's talk later. Okay? I just want to crawl into bed and sleep. I'm tired, and the neighbors are getting an earful," I said, trying to calm him with my gentle tone. If he had asked me this question a few weeks ago, the answer would have been no. Brenden and I had decided to take things slow and not rush into sleeping together again. However, last night things changed.

"No! We are going to discuss this right now," he said, tightening his grip on my arm and halfway dragging me to the door. This wasn't William, not the man I knew. His reaction was seriously scaring me now, and I didn't want the situation to get out of hand and necessitate the involvement of the police.

"Give me your key," he demanded, snatching it from my grasp and struggling to unlock my front door.

"I'm not going to discuss anything while you are acting like you've lost your m-mind," I stuttered, attempting to pull away from him. We struggled for a few seconds.

"Who were you with?"

"I told you."

"Tell me again!"

"An old friend."

"Who? What's his name, Baldwin?"

I didn't answer right away, and he gave me a stern look, like he wasn't playing with me anymore. I figured I had better give him the information he demanded, or the situation might get even uglier. Yet I knew he wouldn't know Brenden from Tom, Dick, or Harry, because I had never mentioned him.

"Brenden," I said, so softly that I didn't recognize my own voice.

"I repeat. Did you fuck him?"

I didn't answer, simply stared at the ground. I couldn't meet his burning gaze, which made me feel like the lowest of the low. And to be honest, I did feel a level of guilt. I wasn't a cheater; I didn't sneak around. My regret was that I hadn't ended my relationship with William before I'd started seeing Brenden again.

"Your lack of an answer says it all, but you are going to give me a level of respect by at least telling me."

"Please, William, let's talk later. You've been drinking, I'm tired, and you are scaring me," I said, backing into my house. "This isn't the time or place."

William snatched me up and literally half carried me into the foyer. He was angrier than I had ever seen him before.

"Did you fuck him?" he asked, squeezing my shoulders until tears flowed and rolled down my cheeks in a steady stream.

"Yes! Yes! I did! Is that what you want to hear?" I prepared myself for his response.

He released me, jerked away like I was a flaming blaze. I stumbled backward.

"You lying, cheating bitch!" he screamed as he leaned back, clenched his fist like he was going to hit me, but stopped himself at the last second.

"I'm sorry," was all I could manage to utter. I couldn't move from the spot I was suddenly frozen in. I felt like I deserved anything William gave me.

"You're sorry? Yeah, that you are," he said, glaring at me like I was a piece of shit stuck on the bottom of his leather shoe. I would never forget that look, and I knew I had hurt him badly. William abruptly walked out my door and slammed it so hard that the walls vibrated.

After William left, I promptly secured the door, just in case he changed his mind and decided to come back. Only then did I slither down the wall and release more tears as I held my knees and rocked back and forth. I sincerely regretted that our relationship had to end that way. He didn't deserve this. For all his faults, William really was a good man and a great catch, just not for me. Talking to and being with Brenden confirmed that.

A couple of hours later, I felt a little better as I lay in bed, talking to Brenden. There was something about him that made me feel that everything was going to be okay when I heard his soothing voice.

"Are you sure he didn't hurt you? Because if he did—"

"No, he didn't, baby. I'm okay. Just a little shook up."

"You sure? You don't sound okay."

"I'm positive. William was just hurt, which he had every right to be. We dated for two years, and I could have handled this situation much better. I, for one, know that you don't play with a person's feelings."

"Well, I'm sorry you were ambushed like that."

"Me too," I said sadly, holding back tears and rubbing the purplish bruise on my tender arm.

"A real man doesn't step to a woman like that. Promise me, if he bothers you again, you'll let me know right away."

"I promise, and have I told you how much I love you?" I asked, abruptly changing the subject. I didn't want to talk about William anymore. I wanted to discuss us, Brenden and me.

"You have, but you can tell me again," Brenden said. "I never tire of hearing it."

"I love you, baby, and I'm so glad you're back in my life. I'm just sad that we've missed out on so many years."

"Ah, music to my ears. I love you too. More than you'll ever know, Baldwin. Get some rest, and I'll talk to you tomorrow. Everything is going to get better. I promise."

"If you say so, then it must be true." I laughed.

"Trust me. All I want to do with the rest of my life is to make you happy."

"Sounds good to me. I won't complain."

"I have to put a smile back on your pretty face."

"See, that's why I love you." I meant it too. I loved me some Brenden. After the huge fight with William, he was able to make me smile and reassure me that he was there for me. I wanted to spend the rest of my life with him.

Shortly afterward, I fell peacefully asleep, with flashbacks of sweet kisses and passionate lovemaking with the man I adored. William was a faint, distant memory. I realized when you've experienced real love, you could never go back to an imitation.

Chapter 39

Brenden

Sometimes I thought my life was destined to be on a collision course for disaster, because despite my best efforts at happiness, things never appeared to work out the way I hoped. Happiness always eluded me; it always was just an inch or two out of reach. I could almost grasp it. Almost.

I should have known from past experience that the past couple of months were too good to be true. Men like me rarely had happily ever after endings, because something or someone always came along to fuck it up. I was convinced nice guys did finish last.

Visiting my soon-to-be ex-wife or having any contact with her, even over the phone, was always like going headfirst into the lion's den. My only bright spot had always been my son, Jordan; he was my world. No matter what was going on in my life, he never failed to put a big smile on my face and joy in my heart.

I should have known something was up when Malia phoned the other evening, requesting that I drop by. It wasn't my weekend to pick up my li'l man. I was more than delighted to spend extra time with him. As soon as I'd drop him off after our weekend visits, my heart would hurt, nearly burst, until next time.

It was a Friday night, around seven-thirty or so, when I rang the doorbell of my house, the one I was still faithfully paying the mortgage on each month. Even though I still had a key, I always felt weird simply barging in. Malia opened the door, smiling, not scowling for once.

"Hi. Come on in."

"Hi. Is Jordan ready?" I asked, looking around for him. I noticed the dinner table was set for two, and Malia was looking like she had taken extra care with her hair and makeup, and she had on a sexy black dress hugging all the right places. I couldn't lie; she was a very attractive woman, with her greatest physical asset being her plump, perfectly shaped ass.

"Can't you at least pretend to care about how I'm doing?" she asked, with her nose wrinkled up like she smelled something funky.

"How are you?" I asked flatly.

"I'm fine. Couldn't be better. And no, Jordan's not ready yet," she snapped as I made my way toward the living room.

"Are you having company? Figured that's why you wanted me to pick Jordan up for the weekend." I didn't have a twinge of anger or jealousy. At this point in the game, I didn't care. I was actually feeling sorry for the dude.

"No. Just you, baby."

"What?" I asked, stopping and glancing back at her, not sure if I had heard correctly.

"I prepared your favorites," she said, suddenly smiling sweetly. "Are you hungry?"

"Thanks, but no thanks. Jordan and I are going to grab a bite at McDonald's and then go to the movies or play video games."

"Brenden. Please."

"I'm sorry, Malia. I'm here to pick up my son, and that's it."

"Our son."

"Whatever. Our son."

"Has it really gotten to this? You can't have dinner with your wife?" she asked, obviously taken aback by my response.

"Soon-to-be ex-wife."

"For right now I'm still your wife, Brenden."

"Here we go again. I'm sorry, Malia. I didn't want to announce it like this, but I want a divorce. You and I both know it will never work. We are over. Have been for quite a while now."

If looks could kill, I would have been dead on the spot. "It's her, isn't it? You were willing to work on our marriage until you went away to that damn funeral."

"What are you talking about?" I asked, suddenly paying close attention.

"I'm not a fool, Brenden. I know you've been seeing her."

"Seeing who?"

"You know exactly who I'm referring to. Baldwin," she spat. "Don't insult my intelligence."

"Who told you that?"

"Never mind all that. I have my sources, and like I said, I'm no fool. You thought you were being so slick, flying back and forth to visit that tramp in Atlanta."

I felt every muscle in my jaw clench up. "First of all, she's not a tramp. Don't call her that again." Hearing her call Baldwin that name made my level of disgust for her rise even higher. I couldn't believe I had wasted so many precious years of my life with this person I felt I didn't really know at times.

"Are you kidding me? Are you really taking up for her?"

"Jordan!"

"He's not here, so you can quit calling him. He spent the night with a playmate, so it's just you and me."

Turning my back on her, I said, "I'm out of here, then. I don't know what you think—"

"I'm pregnant," she said as calmly as if she was saying she was going to the store to pick up a loaf of bread and milk.

I slowly turned around and stared at her in disbelief.

"That's right. I'm pregnant, and you're the daddy. Congratulations!" she spat.

I couldn't move. It was as if Malia had literally punched me in the stomach. I was queasy and light-headed. Spots of light danced in front of my eyes.

"Now, what exactly are you going to do about it?"

"How? When?" I questioned, holding on to the back of the love seat with clenched fingers. She had literally almost brought me to my knees. I felt weak.

"I think you know the answer to both of your questions."

"Damn. I thought you were on the pill."

"You, of all people, should know that it isn't one hundred percent effective."

I buried my face in my hands and moaned. "How could I be so stupid?"

"Again, what are you . . . What are *we* going to do about this?"

I couldn't think straight. The room was spinning out of control. All I could think was, *Not again. Not now.*

"*Our* unborn child deserves for us to try and make our marriage work, Brenden. I've never stopped loving you. Children need their father *and* mother living under the same roof. I don't care what people say. You can't be a full-time daddy living halfway across town, having visitation every other weekend. You're a good father, and you know I'm a good mother. We can go to counseling again, try to work out our differences. You owe our unborn child at least that much."

I was stumbling over my own feet in an attempt to leave. I wasn't sure if my legs would carry me to the door. If not, I intended to crawl. I had to get out of there. I could no longer breathe.

"Where are you going?" she screamed, scrambling to block my path.

"Move, Malia." I barely got out.

"No, we need to talk now. You've let that home wrecker confuse you and mess up your priorities."

"Don't go there! Our marriage was on the rocks long before Baldwin came back into the picture, and you know that."

"Still taking up for that . . . that home-wrecking tramp?"

"Malia, I've warned you to watch your damn mouth. Don't blame the failure of our marriage on anyone but you and me, mostly you."

"Whatever. Run to her defense," Malia said, all up in my face. She was so close, I could feel her hot breath tickle my cheek.

"Move out of my way, Malia."

"Make me move."

"Here we go again. This is exactly why I left your ass to begin with."

"You are damn right. Here we go again. You are going to answer my damn question."

I placed both hands firmly on her shoulders and forcibly pushed her out of my path. "Calm down," I whispered. "I'm going to say this only one time. Listen closely."

I finally had her undivided attention.

"My priorities are in order, and they always have been, so don't come at me talking about what I've let Baldwin do to me. I've lived with you all these years, haven't I? You, with your selfish, deceitful, scheming ways and bad attitude. Nobody but you did this."

"Brenden!" she cried out, reaching for me.

"You brought this on yourself."

"Brenden, come back. This conversation is not over."

"I'll call you later," I cried, storming out the door and not looking back, not once.

Chapter 40

Baldwin

"I'm confused, and I don't know what to do. I can't abandon my unborn child." Brenden had explained that to me two weeks ago, and I had been miserable ever since. It was amazing how one event could turn your world upside down, for the worse.

"Bria, I can't believe this is a repeat of college all over again. Karma comes back strong," I cried into my cell phone from my spot in bed, where I had been for the last two weekends. I somehow managed to make it through work each day, but once I arrived home, I crashed and burned, cried myself to sleep almost every night. I couldn't believe how I always seemed to come out with the short end of the stick.

"That scheming bitch knows his weakness is his children, so once again she traps him. I think we need to fly to Chicago to see ole girl and set her straight," Bria said, serious as a heart attack. "She doesn't know who she is messing with."

I laughed in spite of myself. "Stop it. You're too much, Bria. We will do no such thing."

"At least I got some laughter out of you."

"I know I'm depressing, and I don't mean to lay all my sorrow on your shoulders."

"Please, girl, that's what friends are for. What I don't understand is why Brenden had to take his dick out of his pants to begin with. Hell, they are separated. Translation, no sex."

"He claims she seduced him a couple of weeks before the funeral. They had both been drinking, reminiscing about the good times, and he was seriously considering working it out with her for their son's sake. One thing led to another, and they wound up in bed."

"Damn. So now what?" Bria asked.

"Your guess is as good as mine. I realize I can't take being rejected a second time, but at some level I respect the fact that Brenden loves his children and will sacrifice his happiness for theirs. Isn't that sick of me?"

"No, that's called love, baby. However, his being noble isn't going to keep you warm at night."

I sniffed some more, blew into my tissue, trying to keep another round of tears at bay as I shifted position.

"What is Brenden saying about all of this, Baldwin?"

"Nothing much. He asked me to be patient with him, begging for me to try to understand his position, blah, blah, blah."

"That's bullshit, and Brenden knows it."

"I know, right?"

"Well, are you?"

"To be honest, I don't know what I'm going to do. I can't keep placing my happiness or my heart on hold forever."

"True. I agree. It's not fair to you."

"One thing I learned from Rihanna's death is that life is too short. Brenden and I have been given a second chance at happiness, and now this happens. Maybe we weren't meant to be together. We've had so many struggles in the past. You've witnessed some of the ignorance we've gone through."

"I have, but every relationship has ups and downs."

"This many?" I questioned.

"There is always something, that's life, but I agree that Brenden can't expect you to place your life on hold, waiting on him to reach a decision."

"Bria, I can't go through losing him again. Not now. Not after everything we've been through. I don't know what I'm going to do," I sighed as I reached for the tissue box that sat on the nightstand.

"Whatever you decide, I have your back. Through thick and thin."

"Thanks, Bria. I truly appreciate you. Until we were reunited, I never fully realized or understood what I was missing out on by not having a good female friend in my life."

"Call me if you need me, for anything. You know where I'm at and how to reach me."

I ended the call, feeling slightly better. Bria always knew what to say and was guaranteed to make me laugh. I was glad to have her back in my life. I had missed having a close girlfriend who I could share my thoughts and feelings with. It was as if Bria had never been gone. Our friendship fell right back into place, right where it left off.

Chapter 41

Christopher

"Man, I know you are not going to let Baldwin slip away again. Don't be a fool twice." I couldn't believe the recent turn of events.

Brenden sighed like he had the weight of the world on his shoulders. And I was sure it felt like he did.

"I don't know what I'm going to do. Man, half the time I don't know whether I'm coming or going."

"That's fucked up."

"You know she won't talk to me. It's been a few weeks."

"Who?"

"Baldwin. Who else?"

"Damn, man. Can you blame her?" I wasn't sugar-coating my feelings at this point. My man needed to hear the truth.

"I guess not, but I never told her we would never be together. I simply asked her for some time until I decided what I wanted to do, how I wanted to handle this situation."

I was blown away. "Brenden, be for real. That was another slap in the face to her. What if she waits and you don't choose her? Don't get me wrong. I do understand your predicament and think it's honorable you want to be there for your unborn child, but, man, you can still do that in another household. Your happiness is important too."

I couldn't understand why he just didn't get it. If he didn't make a decision soon, he was going to lose Baldwin. And knowing Baldwin, this time it would be for good. There wouldn't be another chance. At times, I wanted to shake some sense into my man.

I heard another sigh escape. I felt helpless, because both of my friends were in pain and there wasn't anything I could do about it. This was one time I wouldn't want to be in Brenden's shoes. He had some hard decisions to make.

"Don't you think your children will pick up on the fact that you aren't happy?" I asked him.

"I guess you're right."

"I know I am. I grew up with my mom and dad fighting and arguing all the damn time. Like cats and dogs. I would go into my room, put on my headphones, and listen to my rap music to drown out their voices. I was ecstatic when they finally divorced my senior year of high school. I didn't stop loving either one any less because they separated. In fact, I was thrilled they had finally found their happiness, apart from each other. Looking back, that's probably why I grew up so fucked up in the relationship department. My dad, my role model, was a chronic cheater and womanizer, man."

"I hear you, and I understand what you're saying. I just have to think about all of this and put it into perspective."

"Knowing Baldwin, she is not going to wait around for your ass forever."

"I know."

"Can I ask you something?"

"Sure."

"Does Baldwin make you happy?"

"Happier than I've been in a long time."

"Have you forgiven her from years ago?"

"Of course. We were young, and she wasn't ready for that type of responsibility. I realize that now."

"Have you forgiven yourself? Maybe you think you could have done something to stop her from having an abortion. I know I'm grasping at straws here, playing amateur shrink."

"You think I'm a mental patient? Is that what you're saying?" he joked.

"No, I understand this is hard for you, and I'd hate to be in your shoes with such a critical decision to make."

"I think the best decision was made for us back then, whether I realized it or not."

"Well then, don't you deserve happiness? Do you want to continue to exist in a perpetual state of unhappiness?"

Later, Brenden told me that that question had haunted him for the rest of the day. He said that when he really stepped back and took a good look at his life, he realized he was always trying to make someone else happy. He was constantly looking out for someone else. Continuously placing himself second best to take care of someone else's needs first. Even his chosen profession placed him in the role of looking out for the less fortunate. He had never truly thought about what he wanted and needed and, mostly, deserved.

Chapter 42

Baldwin

It had been almost a month since I last spoke with Brenden, and my heart was broken—it literally ached. Yet I refused to play second fiddle anymore. I had done that with William and in previous relationships, always trying to satisfy the other person's needs and not looking out for my own. As much as I loved Brenden, never again.

Speaking of William, we got back together temporarily, very briefly. William and I ran into each other at Lenox Mall, and for a moment, I was truly happy to see him, even after everything that had occurred between us. I started thinking that maybe we could have worked out our differences. It wasn't fair to him that I had subconsciously compared our relationship to the one I shared with Brenden years ago. I realized that was my problem. All my past relationships never had a chance from the very beginning because I always likened them to what Brenden and I shared in college. There was no comparison, so they were doomed from the start.

"Hello, Baldwin. You're looking lovely, as usual."

"Thank you. How are you, William?" I asked shyly.

"I could be better. Working all the time, but that's nothing new. That hasn't changed."

Awkward silence followed.

"I've missed you. Baldwin. I've thought about you and how I treated you that morning."

I looked down, shifted my packages around in my hands.

"No matter how angry I was, I shouldn't have put my hands on you. My mama didn't raise me to be that man. I'm sincerely sorry, and I hope you will accept my apology."

I nodded.

"Are you content in your new relationship? I sincerely want you to be happy. You're a good woman, Baldwin."

I hesitated for a few seconds. "Well, actually, we aren't together anymore."

"Damn, that was quick," he said. I knew he was probably secretly pleased. I think I even detected a small smirk on his lips.

"Yeah. I guess it was."

"Well, he was a fool to let you go, because I miss you and realize what I've lost. I also realize how much I took you for granted. I was always putting my job before you and our relationship."

"Thank you for saying that. I needed to hear that, William."

"It's true. I made a lot of mistakes, but I've grown from knowing you. I hope we can remain friends. May I call you sometime? That would mean a lot to me."

I nodded. "Sure." I think I even managed a smile.

At the time, I thought William was simply making small talk. I never thought he would actually take me up on my offer, because I knew William. And I knew that his bed hadn't been empty since our breakup. He understood he was handsome, charming, and a man with a good job and six-figure salary. He was a great catch to many women in Atlanta. However, by the end of the next week, William was calling me nearly every evening to chat for a few minutes. The following week, we went to dinner at a fabulous Moroccan restaurant in Buckhead, complete with belly dancers performing, and slept together the same night. We were caught up in our old roles, and it felt familiar, safe, and secure.

But that still didn't make it love.

Chapter 43

Baldwin

Bria and I were hanging out at my house, lounging, eating, and talking. We had been for the last couple of days. She had phoned a few days earlier and, during the course of our conversation, had asked if she could visit. She said she wanted a change of scenery and what better place than Hotlanta, but I knew she was really afraid of my state of mind and wanted to check on me.

"I am beyond confused, and I feel my life is in total shambles. I don't have the strength to pick up the pieces."

"You'll get past this. Tell me, have you heard from William?" she asked.

"No, I think we both realized it was over. We tried to make it work again, getting back into our old roles and habits. When I broke it off this last time, he didn't even try to persuade me to give us another chance. He simply left and wished me the best."

"To be honest, I'm glad he's out of your life. After you told me what went down that first time, I was scared for you. I don't trust a man who will manhandle a woman the way he did."

"That wasn't the real William I knew. William tried, but he was no Brenden."

"I hear you," Bria chimed in, stretched out on my sofa, sipping a glass of red wine. Bria and I had on our pj's. It was almost ten o'clock, and we were settled in for the night. "But did *you* hear what you just said?"

"It's true. No man can ever measure up to Brenden, and I finally figured it out."

"And what is that?"

"I understand why I have never been truly happy in a relationship for most of my adult life. I've never been treated badly in any of my previous relationships, but I always felt like something was missing and I could never quite put my finger on it. So I always ended up putting more into the relationship than my boyfriend did."

"My Baldwin, my Baldwin. What am I going to do with you?"

"I couldn't tell you," I said in a pitiful voice. I wanted to crawl under a rock and die.

"I'm determined to get you out of this funk before I leave. I wish I could click my heels and make it all better," Bria said.

"Well, you have quite a feat on your hands," I said, glancing down at my fingernails, badly in need of a manicure.

"I'm up for it. I still have a day and a half before I leave. As much as I adore Brenden, don't get me wrong, but he isn't the end all and be all. There are other fish in the sea, my dear Baldwin."

"I've never enjoyed fishing. Too many nasty mosquitoes and lots of sitting and waiting for things to happen. And then the majority of the time, you have to throw them back," I said, shifting position on the opposite end of the sofa from Bria. "I just want my life back. I'm sick of all this drama, because I don't do well with drama. I'm not used to getting late-night threatening phone calls."

"Don't get me started, girl! I'm so pissed about what you told me earlier. I still think you should inform Brenden of what his crazy-ass wife did."

"That will never happen. I haven't talked to Brenden and don't intend to. That will happen when hell freezes over. Every other day he will text or e-mail me. 'I love you, Baldwin. Please be patient with me. I can't lose you again. Our love will overcome this test, and we'll get through this. I can't live without you.' I've even received sappy cards in the mail and had my favorite flowers delivered. I never even consider responding. In fact, I resent him for sending them. Don't send me e-mails and texts. Remedy the situation. Hell, take some action. Actions speak louder than words."

Bria grunted and shifted position.

"Besides, what is there to say? It's almost two months now, and he hasn't made a decision. Besides, even if he chose me, do I really want a man who has to think about being with me?" At that point, I was totally disgusted with Brenden for putting me through this.

Bria shrugged her shoulders and popped a large red seedless grape into her mouth. "What exactly did his skank of a wife say? You never did give me the full, juicy details on all that went down," she said.

"Yes, I did."

"Well, tell me again," she said, giving me her full attention.

"My phone rang a few nights ago, around two o'clock in the morning. I was fast asleep, and I blindly reached for it, not paying attention to the phone number display." I paused.

"Go on. Don't keep me in suspense."

"As soon as I said hello, still groggy from sleep, *she* went off on me. Called me all these foul names. Home wrecker, whore, bitch. It took me totally off guard, and it took me a few moments to wake up before I realized who she was."

"Baldwin, it couldn't have been me. Girl, I would have jumped through that phone and beat the shit out of her ass. I would have snatched her teeth out her mouth and bitch slapped her into next year."

I laughed.

"You laugh, but I'm serious."

"Bria, I don't know what came over me. I literally snapped. I proceeded to call her everything but a child of God. I surprised myself, didn't even think I had it in me. I wouldn't let her get a word in edgewise, and then I simply hung up on her stupid ass."

"It's about time. Good for you, but I still say we should fly to Chicago, rent a car, and go whip her funky butt. She can't be calling up my friend and upsetting her."

"We are going to beat up a pregnant woman?"

"Hell, yeah! I don't have a problem with it. She's supposed to be bad."

I shook my head and laughed again in spite of myself. "Listen, Bria, thanks for flying in to check up on me. I'm glad you're here. It's like old times again. I appreciate you."

"That's what friends do, girl. When you hurt, I hurt."

"I'm going to make it through this. I surely am. This too shall pass," I said, more to myself than to Bria.

Chapter 44

Brenden

A year and a half after Rihanna's funeral . . .

I couldn't do it. Absolutely could not. I couldn't go another single day without Baldwin in my life. Her refusal to talk to me hurt my heart to a degree I couldn't handle. A little over two months was too long for us to be separated, it felt like an eternity, and the only thing I knew for sure, without a shadow of a doubt, was that I loved Baldwin. When I finally came to my senses, I hopped on the first Delta flight, flew into Atlanta, and begged for her forgiveness and promised on my life that I would never leave her side again. And I hadn't. We'd been inseparable.

There was always that one woman who completed you and complemented you all at the same time. Baldwin was that woman for me. She could stroll into a room and I just melted. That was my baby. My heart overflowed with pure love for her, and I was never letting go again. Baldwin was my alpha and omega. I didn't need anyone else, and I was proud to call her my woman, my wife.

Illinois law didn't require you to be separated before you could file for divorce, and Malia and I had been separated well over eight months at the time. So we divorced under irreconcilable differences, and Baldwin

and I made it official. We were Mr. and Mrs. Bailey.
Our impromptu eloping to Vegas didn't set well with
our family and friends, but they forgave us when we
had a huge reception and invited everyone and partied
until the wee hours of the morning. Baldwin simply
glowed. She was breathtaking. And I was the happiest
man on earth at that moment.

Even though I had gone back to Baldwin, I came to
find out Malia had been faking the entire pregnancy. She
claimed she had a miscarriage and lost the baby, but I
didn't believe her for a minute. There never was a baby.
Nevertheless, I made an effort to co-parent with her for
the sake of Jordan. Even though I was living in Atlanta
now, we made it work. I had a lot of frequent-flier miles
flying between Atlanta and Chicago. And believe it or
not, now that she had a new man, Dennis, in her life, she
was not so much of a bitch. She even smiled sometimes.
He was a schoolteacher that she met on a blind date, set
up by one of her girlfriends. I had to admit, he seemed
like a decent guy, and I wouldn't have it any other way
with him spending time with my son.

Life was good. Hell, it was better than good. I had the
woman of my dreams, whom I loved with all my heart
and soul, and a wonderful son, whom I had joint custody of. My life was everything I had dreamt it could be.

Chapter 45

Baldwin

These days a genuine smile was a constant companion on my face. Life with Brenden was beyond the happiness that I thought it would be. I simply beamed. I counted my blessings that we had found each other again. I never realized I could be so content as a wife, lover, and friend. I could honestly say marriage definitely agreed with me on many levels.

Brenden had resigned from his job, given up living in Chicago to relocate to Atlanta to be with me, had found a new job, and now had joint custody of his son. It had been two years now since we'd eloped, and we were still behaving like honeymooners. We couldn't keep our hands off one another. We still acted silly and giggled and made love like it was going out of style; we couldn't get enough of one another. Brenden inspired me to be a better person, to do my best, to follow my dreams, and lead with my heart. It brought great joy to know that he always had my back and vice versa. Life couldn't get much better.

Brenden and I kept the lines of communication completely open, and we talked a lot, shared our feelings. Like last night. I was lying next to Brenden, both of us totally nude, in our usual spooning position. "I love you, Brenden," I announced, then waited for his standard reply.

"I love you more," he replied, kissing along the side of my neck, near my earlobe.

I shivered. "You know that's my sweet spot. Don't be starting something you can't finish, baby."

"Oh, I can finish it, all right. Want me to show you again?"

"No, baby. Not yet, anyway," I teased. "You're insatiable."

"For you."

"You're sweet."

"You're beautiful. Besides, we have to continue to practice so that we'll create our perfect little girl or boy."

I smiled and pushed my body closer to his, if that was possible. "I am ready to experience being pregnant and having a baby."

"I know you are. You are great with Jordan, and he loves you."

"And I love him too. He's the spitting image of his daddy, so what's not to adore? He has such a caring spirit, like someone else I know."

"I'm so proud of the young man he's growing into."

"Did you believe we could be this happy?" I asked

"Yes. You and I together, that's all I've ever wanted. We are unstoppable."

"How many babies are we going to have?" I asked, enjoying our closeness and intimate conversation.

"An entire houseful, if that's what you want." He laughed, snuggling closer. We meshed into one.

"Have you have lost your mind?"

Brenden laughed again. "Seriously, at least two. Don't you think?" he asked.

"Two is a good number."

"A girl for you to dote on and dress up, and I'd also like another son. With Jordan, we'll be complete."

"I like how that sounds. Complete."

"It does sound nice," he said, reaching around to caress my breasts with even, gentle strokes.

"You complete me, and I don't know how I ever lived without you. I've never been this happy and at peace," I cooed. "Never knew I could be."

"Come here," he said, climbing between my legs and lavishing my face with fresh kisses. "Prove it."

When he slowly eased himself inside, I closed my eyes and exhaled. I finally knew what Terry McMillan was talking about in her book *Waiting to Exhale*. I was no longer waiting or inhaling. We made love into the early morning hours, not worried about time, bursting with our hopes and dreams for the future and our new-found life together.

However, the joke was on us. Life could be cruel.

Chapter 46

Baldwin

Bad things could and did happen to good people. I was an eyewitness. *It* happened on a rainy, cold Friday night not long after a joyous Thanksgiving celebration.

The call came. There was something about that ringing phone that I would never forget. It was like I knew. Don't ask me how. I literally broke out in a cold sweat before I even picked up the receiver. One chain of events could completely change your life forever.

"Hello?" I asked with shaky, trembling hands.

"May I speak with Baldwin Bailey?" asked the voice on the other end of the line.

"This is she. Who's calling?"

"I'm calling from Emory University Hospital, and we . . ."

I think I cried out even before the soft-spoken woman on the line could finish her sentence.

"What? Why? What's happened? What is this about?" I asked, protectively clutching my six-month pregnant stomach as the baby kicked.

"I need you to calm down," the woman said in a reassuring, tranquil voice. "Your husband, Brenden Bailey, has been involved in a traffic accident, and we need you to come to Emory University Hospital as soon as possible."

"Oh my God! Is he all right? May I speak with him?" I questioned in rushed sentences.

"Mr. Bailey's doctor will discuss that with you and answer any questions you may have upon your arrival. Is there anyone who can drive you?"

"No, but I'm on my way."

I didn't recall hanging up; to be honest, I didn't even recall the drive over. I drove on autopilot. Thank goodness the hospital was only about twenty minutes from our home. My only thought was getting to Brenden, being by his side. I sobbed the entire drive over. I hadn't even bothered to grab a coat or umbrella.

When I arrived, cold, shivering, and drenched, Dr. Shahr, a thin, balding, middle-aged Indian physician, briefed me on Brenden's condition. He had been in a major car accident. Three other vehicles were involved, and there were seriously injured passengers, two DOA. Brenden was in a coma. Dr. Shahr explained how the first twenty-four to forty-eight hours would be very important and he would be monitored closely.

My mind immediately went back to a conversation Brenden and I had earlier that day, around noon.

"Hey, baby. How's my big baby and my small one doing?"

"We're fine. She has been kicking a lot today," I said, rubbing my belly. Yes, we were having a girl.

"She just misses her daddy's voice. That's all. I haven't sung to her in a couple of days," Brenden said.

I smiled lovingly. Brenden was forever laying his head on my stomach and talking and singing nursery rhymes to our baby. He did it every day, religiously, and she would literally kick and move around, as if in response.

"How are you, baby? How is the conference going? Are you finished with the breakout sessions?" I asked. When he relocated to Atlanta, he had no problem getting a job at one of the major nonprofits. So he was still giving back and making a difference.

"It's going well, but I'm tired. I still have a few more hours to go before I can wrap it up and get out of here."

"I thought you were coming home tomorrow, baby?"

"I'm finishing up earlier than expected, and I really just want to get home tonight. Sleep in my own bed, snuggled up next to my beautiful wife."

"That's sweet, but seriously, I don't mind if you stay one more night. I'll be fine, and you said yourself that you are tired. Get some rest."

"I am worn-out, but I hate staying away from you too long. Especially now."

"Well, I guess I'll see you tonight."

Brenden and I talked a bit more and then said our good-byes since the conference's fifteen-minute break had ended. If only he had taken my advice and stayed one more night. I should have insisted he not drive home until the next day, because I knew those conferences could be draining. If only . . .

"Where is he? I need to see him. Right now," I insisted.

"Do you have anyone here with you?" the doctor asked. I guess he saw the panic-stricken look on my face.

"No. I rushed straight over when I received the call," I said, breathing rapidly and holding my stomach.

"Okay, I need you to calm down. Neither your husband nor your unborn baby needs you all worked up."

I nodded, took a deep breath, and followed the doctor. He had warned me not to be alarmed at how Brenden looked, but I was. I literally gasped and felt weak at the knees. I had to clutch the doctor's arm to keep from falling. There were wires and tubes everywhere the eyes could behold. And my baby looked so frail lying in that hospital bed with bandages snugly wrapped around his head.

I walked over and picked up his right hand, kissed it, and enclosed it in mine, brought it to my heart.

"Baby, I'm here. I promise everything is going to be all right. We've been through too much together for you to leave me now. I love you so much. This is just another storm we have to get through together."

That became my routine. I didn't leave his side. I held Brenden's hand, gently massaged it, and talked to him. I talked to him about nothing and everything. Just talked. About our dreams, our future, our love. Brenden was my sole, single focus, even though I was aware that I needed to take care of myself for our unborn baby's sake.

"Baby, your doctors say there's a good possibility that you can hear me. I feel that you can. I know that you realize I'm here by your side. We are a team, a good team, and we'll beat this together.

"You have to wake up and get better so you can talk to our baby girl. She has been kicking and moving around, waiting for you to sing to her. What is that nursery rhyme you sing? I've been thinking of some more baby names too, and I need you to tell me which ones you like. I know you are going to balk at some of the names I chose. Do you like Alexis? What about Alexandra? Brittany? Wake up, baby. I need you."

At news of the accident, Bria and Christopher flew in and were by my side. I didn't ask them to come. They simply did. I refused to leave the hospital, so they made sure I ate and took care of the baby and myself. They respected the fact that I needed alone moments as well. So they let me be during those times when I was on the brink of breaking down. I'd catch them looking at me now and then with worried, weary eyes. I had never been so scared and apprehensive in my entire life, but my angels lifted me up when I was down and gave me a shoulder, two shoulders, to lean on and cry on.

Since I refused for Brenden to be alone for even a minute, when I took small breaks, when I was too overcome with emotion, Bria or Christopher sat in the room and talked to him. I refused to let him wake up and find no one there for him. I wanted him to feel a familiar presence in the room with him at all times. I played his favorite songs on his CD player and talked about what was on TV or spoke about how his friends and coworkers who came by were doing. Like mine, his parents were deceased.

Many times I walked into the hospital room and found Christopher talking to him about something that happened when they were roommates. Christopher had many good stories, fun experiences they had shared.

Or sometimes I'd find Bria laughing and joking with him about how she couldn't wait until he woke up so she could kid him about how puke-green hospital gowns didn't complement his complexion. Even though I saw the sorrow in her eyes, Bria cut up with Brenden as if he could hear every word she said. And I imagined he did and was silently laughing inside, just cracking up over her antics.

During those moments, I realized the power of true friendship and the beauty of love. A cocoon of love for my man and for my friends embraced me and kept me sane.

I went through many emotions during those three days. I cried, I laughed, I cherished our memories, I prayed, prayed some more at the small chapel in the hospital, but through it all, I tried to remain strong. It was probably the hardest thing I ever had to do, but I knew Brenden would want me to be brave and strong, for his sake and for our baby's.

After much effort, I was kneeling on my knees, hands together, eyes closed, and head bowed in prayer. I was back at the tiny chapel, which was a source of comfort.

"Dear God, I know you haven't heard from me on a regular basis up until now, but I'm here and I know you haven't forgotten me. You said you would never forsake your children and would never leave us. I need you to hear my plea, Lord. I need you, Jesus, to perform healing miracles. I need you to give me strength to carry on through this tribulation.

"I'm so, so, so scared. Lord, you have to bless and protect my husband. He's such a good man, a kind man. Brenden is the love of my life, and I can't live without him, not again. We finally reunited and we're happy. My heart overflows with pure love. And our baby is going to complete our family in a few months. Brenden is so excited. We both are.

"He's not doing well. The doctors aren't coming right out and saying it, but it's touch and go. They are waiting to determine the extent of his injuries until after the swelling goes down on his brain, and they don't know how much, if any, brain damage he might have. I can't lose him, Lord. I just can't. If you can raise the dead, you can heal my husband. If anything happens to him, I don't know what I'll do. I don't know if I'll be able to go on. He's my life. And Lord, please bless Bria and Christopher, my angels on earth. I'm so thankful for them. All these things I ask in Jesus's name. Amen."

On the fourth day, Brenden did something miraculous. He opened his eyes. I sent silent prayers straight to heaven. Later, his doctors would say they had rarely seen that happen before, not with the injuries he had sustained. It was a miracle. Brenden was my miracle.

I was sitting in my usual spot, in the dark brown recliner within inches of his bed. I remember feeling the baby give me an extremely harsh kick, and I glanced down to gently rub my stomach. When I looked up, Brenden was simply staring at me with a look of confusion on his face, trying to speak. I think I stopped breathing for a second as my heart leapt into my throat. I was so choked up with emotion and so grateful. I jumped up, elated.

"Oh, Brenden, I knew you'd come back to us!" I cried out, hugging him, kissing his face, and pushing the call button for a nurse all at the same time. I was so happy. Tears of joy streamed down my face in hot trails.

I could tell he was trying to speak, but his throat was too dry. Within seconds, two nurses rushed into the room, and his doctor was immediately called. I smiled back at him as I was swiftly ushered out.

I was so ecstatic, I didn't know what to do with myself. I called Christopher and Bria with the good news, and I could feel their happiness seeping through the phone. They had been staying at our home since arriving in town, helping with household responsibilities, putting in shifts at the hospital and being godsends.

Hours passed before I was allowed back into Brenden's room. It seemed like an eternity. I was told that he didn't remember anything about the accident, that he would probably sleep a lot, and they were waiting on preliminary tests results they had taken.

During my wait, I sent even more praises and thanks up to heaven. When I was finally allowed back in the room, Brenden was quietly resting in bed after all the tests had been performed. Some of the wires and tubes, not all, had been removed. I was overjoyed to see him awake. If my love was tangible, it would have filled up the entire room, leaving not an ounce of space. He painfully turned his head in my direction, as if sensing my presence. I could tell he was in pain and trying not to show it.

I put on a strong facade and smiled, walked over to kiss his cheek.

"Welcome back, baby. Don't ever scare us like that again."

"Hey," he said with some difficulty.

"You had us scared for a minute. Are you in any pain?" I asked, looking into his face for clues.

He tried to talk. I could tell he was extremely weak based on his slow movements; he also appeared to be in a state of confusion. I was told that was typical for coma patients.

"Don't talk, baby. Just nod yes or no."

He shook his head to indicate he wasn't in pain. However, I was pretty certain he was lying so that I wouldn't worry about him even more. I knew the doctor was giving him pain medication due to his serious injuries.

"Everything is going to be okay now. I want you to rest, save your strength, and get better. In case you have forgotten, we are having a baby in three months."

He attempted a smile as I snuggled next to him on the bed and held his hand. He was asleep within minutes. And that was how it went for the next couple of days. Brenden was in and out. Sometimes he would fall asleep in the midst of a sentence and would sleep for hours. Sometimes he would wake up confused, and at other times with clarity.

"How's our b—baby?" he managed to stammer the next day.

"Busy as ever, kicking and moving around."

"Feisty," he muttered. "Just like her mama."

The next morning I gave him great news when he woke up. "Baby, Christopher and Bria are on their way to visit you, with Jordan. However, I want you to keep it short and sweet. I don't want them tiring you out. Save your strength for getting better."

He nodded slightly.

"I love you, Brenden. I love you with all my heart."

"I know. And I love you back."

The doctor had made it very clear not to wear him out and for the visits to be short. Those who couldn't visit sent well wishes. His room was filled with balloons, flowers, and get-well cards from family, friends, and coworkers.

Jordan and his mom had flown in the night before and had stayed at a nearby hotel, even though I had offered my home. Malia didn't want to be a bother and had insisted that they would be fine at a hotel. The situation had been explained to Jordan, but not too much detail had been given, even though he was almost thirteen now. I had warned Malia about the tubes and bandages and that it might be frightening to him, so she had tried to prepare him without upsetting him.

Jordan walked in with me from the lobby, a bit unsure when he saw Brenden lying in bed. Jordan had grown even taller since the last time I saw him.

"Hey, Dad," he said quietly.

"Hey, buddy," Brenden managed to say with a slight smile. His eyes shone with love.

"Dad, are you going to be all right?" he questioned, looking anxiously from Brenden to me. "I heard you were in a bad car accident."

"Like your mother told you, your dad doesn't feel well right now, but he's going to get well soon, if his doctors and I have anything to do with it. Okay?" I said reassuringly.

"Okay," Jordan said, looking at me as if holding me to that promise.

"I know you are a preteen now, but you can give your dad a hug and kiss and tell him you love him if you'd like." I tried to keep my voice steady and calm.

He nodded, looking just like his daddy with those big, innocent eyes. This broke my heart.

"I'm sure he will love that, but you have to remember to be careful, Jordan. Be real gentle," I added.

Jordan walked over to the bed, and in order to give them some privacy, I went into the bathroom to fill a plastic pitcher with water to pour into the flower vases.

"I love you, Dad," he said with a voice full of emotion. He bent down to hug and kiss Brenden on the cheek.

Brenden held him close and tight. "I love you too," Brenden said as he quickly turned his head, with tears in his eyes, to face the other wall.

"Jordan, your dad is so happy to see you, but I think he's getting a little tired. So let's allow him to get some rest. All right?" I said, walking over, giving him a hug. "You can visit again later."

"Okay," he said, his eyes watering up.

I noticed Brenden trying to speak again. "Be good. I love you, son. I'm very proud of you."

"I will, Daddy," Jordan answered, and he turned to walk out the door, then suddenly stopped and waved good-bye like he was six years old again. "Get well, Dad."

After Jordan's visit, Brenden became very quiet. He slept a lot afterward, and I stayed by his side to watch over him. I would never forget coming back into the room later that evening, after Christopher and Bria had visited with Brenden. He had awakened and had asked to see them privately. After saying their good nights, I noticed they were unusually quiet and subdued as they headed to the bank of elevators. However, I didn't comment and pushed it to the back of my mind.

Brenden was softly crying when I reentered the room.

"What's wrong, baby? I asked, rushing to his side. "Are you in pain? Do you need me to call a nurse?"

"No, I'm fine," he said, almost in a whisper. I had to lean my head toward his mouth to hear his words.

"What's wrong, then?" I asked, wiping away his tears with my fingertips. "You are going to make me cry. Tell me. What upset you?"

He paused. "I'm thinking about how much I'm going to miss you."

I stood straight up, shocked.

"Baby, don't say that. You're not going anywhere but home, where you belong. You are going to be fine. What would make you say that?"

"Shhh, listen to me, Baldwin. Make sure my daughter knows me, and look after my son. Keep him in your life," he said with great difficulty, but with determination.

"Brenden, don't. Why are you talking like this?" I said, tears starting to fall as my body trembled uncontrollably.

"Don't cry, Baldwin. I need you to be strong. I've talked to Bria and Christopher, and they know my wishes in case anything happens to me. I want to make sure everything is in order, just in case."

"We're going to get through this. I can't lose you again, baby."

He shook his head and closed his eyes before continuing. "Listen to me. I spoke with my primary doctor, along with Christopher and Bria, and my brain trauma caused serious secondary injuries. I'm not getting any better. I'm actually getting worse, and I refuse to be hooked up to any machine, and I'm too weak for any operations. I didn't want to upset you and risk complications with your pregnancy, so I asked them not to say anything to you."

"I don't believe it. Let's get a second opinion," I said, already moving toward the door. "Doctors don't always get it right."

"Baldwin, please, I need you to be strong."

"You are not getting worse."

"Baby, I am. I can feel myself slipping away."

"I can't lose you, Brenden."

"I'll always be with you. I'll always watch over you."

I shook my head and moaned.

"Baldwin, I need you to be strong," he said with a quivering voice. "This is why I didn't want to tell you."

"Okay," I said, attempting to calm down for his sake.

"Good." He attempted a small smile. "That's my girl."

"I love you," I managed to say.

"You've been the best thing that ever happened to me, Baldwin."

"You too."

"I want you to live your life and be truly happy. I'll always be with you, but don't give up on love. Keep your heart open. It'll find you again."

With those words, I walked over to his bed, pulled a chair up to it, sat, and laid my head on his stomach and cried like a baby.

"I need to know you'll be all right, Baldwin. I'm so tired, but I can't be at peace until I know you and the baby will be all right. Don't mourn me. Be thankful for the time we had together. I am."

With those words, something snapped inside. A sense of peace overcame me, and I stopped crying. I had to be tough, realizing these might be my last moments with the love of my life. Evidently, he knew something I didn't. He was holding on for me.

For most of the night, I lay in bed next to him, in his arms. I talked, talked of happy times together. Brenden didn't say much more. He simply listened. He had had his say, and I believed he was at peace.

Two days later, right as dawn crested upon the horizon, he slipped quietly away. Like the calm, peaceful spirit he was, just like that, he was gone. I sensed it before I confirmed it.

I knew the instant he left me; something in my spirit told me so. It was like my soul split in two. I sat with him, holding his hand for a while before the nurse came in. He looked peaceful and free. Mostly, he looked loved. I sat and reflected on how happy he had made me. I regretted how we had been given a second chance, only to have it end this way. Life was so unfair. I had experienced so much death during my lifetime: my parents, grandparents, Rihanna, and now my beloved husband. I had never felt so alone and bitter.

Looking back I didn't know how I made it through the next few days. I guess I ran on pure adrenaline. However, I kept my promise to Brenden and remained strong.

Chapter 47

Baldwin

The funeral was held four days later, on a dark, dreary, gloomy afternoon. Dressed in black, family and friends from far and wide attended to say their final good-byes. The church was packed to capacity, with standing room only.

I sat numb between Bria and Christopher, shrouded in a daze throughout most of the service. It didn't go unnoticed by me that the group was shrinking and nothing would ever be the same. It used to be Bria, Rihanna, and I flanked and protected by Brenden and Christopher. Now there was only Christopher and Bria. I went through the motions and took in portions of the service and the kind words. One conclusion I came away with and would always cherish was that my husband was loved, loved by many. The many flowers, testimonies, and attendees were evidence of that. He had touched many lives during his short tenure on earth.

"Is there anyone else who'd like to share a few words concerning our dearly beloved brother?" our reed-thin pastor asked, searching the crowd with his eyes.

On autopilot, I found myself rising and walking to the front of the church. People started whispering, anticipating what I was going to say. Christopher tried to stop me, but Bria nudged him away. She told him to let me speak.

As I stood in the pulpit and looked out into the congregation at the ocean of expectant faces, the words simply flowed. Gushed straight from the heart and, I imagined, streamed up to heaven. I sensed Brenden's spirit by my side, and I embraced it.

"Not too long ago, I attended another funeral. It was the home going of a very dear friend, and I walked away with the realization that life is short. I made a commitment on that day to live my life to the fullest. At the time, I never in a million years would have thought I'd be married, pregnant, and burying my husband a little over four years later. Fairy tales aren't supposed to end in a nightmare.

"Brenden was the love of my life, and it seemed like we went through hell and back to be together. You just don't know, but through it all we were together, married for over three years. Three of the most unbelievable, wonderful, unforgettable years of my life. I loved him so much, and I know without a shadow of a doubt that he loved me back. He proved it every day he breathed, in small and large ways.

"There were ignorant, small-minded people who didn't want us to be together simply because of the color of our skin. They frowned upon our union, but you see, love overcame all that. Love is pure. Love is color blind. We couldn't help who we fell in love with. When I looked at Brenden, I didn't see a white man. All I saw was unconditional love and a man who cherished me, this African American woman.

"I'm carrying his baby, a baby girl that he named on his deathbed. She'll grow up knowing and adoring her father, just as I did and always will. She won't care that her daddy was white and she's the biracial product of our love. She'll learn that it is all about the character and heart of a person. That tells the true story. Our unborn child and Brenden's son, Jordan, will carry on his legacy. My husband touched many lives, which are better because of knowing him. Pray for us. Please pray for us."

As I walked back to my seat and right into the warm embrace of my two best friends, I didn't know what the future held, but I suddenly realized I would survive somehow.

Epilogue

Baldwin

A year later . . .

My baby girl, McKenzie, saved my life. I could honestly say that I didn't know if I would have been able to go on if it hadn't been for her. I never imagined I could love someone other than Brenden the way I loved her. I cherished her with an undeniable motherly passion. And I saw Brenden all over her, from her eyes to her easy smile to her mild demeanor. She was my heart. One day, when she was older, I was going to tell her our story, the story of her mother and father. The story of when Baldwin loved Brenden.

I thought it was love at first sight for her and Jordan. He adored her. He was crazy about his little sister and was a constant in her life. Malia realized it was senseless to deprive Jordan of his connection to his baby sibling. I certainly wouldn't say Malia and I became best friends overnight, but we made it work, for the sake of our children. Jordan visited whenever possible, and that was often.

I couldn't begin to say enough about Bria and Christopher. They literally moved in after the funeral. Bria took a leave of absence from her job and stayed with me throughout the remainder of my pregnancy. Terry came every other weekend. Bria made sure I looked

after the baby and myself. Made sure I ate, took show-
ers, and combed my hair . . . things I couldn't quite get
myself to do with Brenden gone. What was the point?
Even though we cried together, she wouldn't allow me
to wallow in self-pity, and she even shared a bit of what
Brenden had told her on his deathbed. Even then, my
baby was thinking of me. He wanted me to eventually
find love again and be happy.

After the baby was born, Christopher stayed with
me for a while, commuting back and forth. I realized
it caused tension with his girlfriend, but he insisted on
staying and wouldn't have it any other way. Since he
didn't have a traditional job, his office was anywhere
he set up a PC and phone. I would never forget that
act of unselfishness for as long as I lived. I loved Bria
and Christopher so much; words couldn't even begin
to describe it. Of course, they were the godparents to
our baby. They had shown me what a difference true
friends could make in your life, especially during times
of heartache. I would do anything for them with no
hesitation.

Bria became a mother herself. The adoption finally
came through for her and Terry, and they'd had their
baby girl for six months now. Bria was a great mother,
which I knew she would be. So our girls would grow up
together, and I thought that was absolutely cool. That
placed a genuine smile on my face.

Christopher got married. It was a long, long time
coming, but he finally jumped the broom. He hung in
there. I thought he and Tamara would live together forever without making it official. I never believed I would
see the day that a woman made an honest man out of
him. He was happy. And I was happy for him, for them.
Marriage was good for him. He had a lovely wife who
had earned her title and wore it well. I swear, on the

day of the wedding, I felt Brenden's spirit all around us. Christopher even had an empty chair placed at the groom's table in his honor.

The circle of life and death had completed itself.

The last year had been full of many joys and pains and challenges. I missed Brenden and thought of him always. I felt his spirit all around, especially around our daughter. Protecting and loving, guiding, and being proud of us.

At first I questioned and cursed God as to how He could be so cruel as to give us such a short time together. Oh, how I cursed Him. I couldn't even attend church anymore. How could I worship such a cruel, heartless God? Then one morning, after waking from a peaceful dream, one in which Brenden visited, I realized I had it all wrong. I should be thanking God for the three-plus years He gave us together as man and wife. I should have been thanking Him for placing such a wonderful man in my life, one who taught me about love and forgiveness, and one who gave me the greatest gift of all—our daughter.

I was now taking it one day at a time, one step at a time. My mother was right; one step at a time would get you through. Life was short, and I was going to make the most of it. Rejoice in every day, in every breath I took. Brenden and Rihanna would want it that way.

Questions for Discussion

1. Have you ever experienced the loss of a really good friend? If so, how did you handle your grief?

2. Is it possible to rekindle a friendship after many years have passed with little contact?

3. Was college some of the best days of your life? Did you establish lifelong friendships?

4. What were your initial thoughts of Rihanna, Baldwin, Brenden, Bria, and Christopher?

5. What were the group's dynamics?

6. Did Baldwin truly love Brenden and vice versa?

7. Can love really conquer all?

8. Who was your favorite character, and why?

9. Which character and issue could you identify with the most?

10. Do you think the friendships will remain strong?

11. What did you think of the twist at the end of the novel? Were you surprised?

12. Where do you see Baldwin and the rest of the group in five years?